Acclaim For the Wo

MAX ALLAN COLLINS!

D0601172

"Crime fiction aficionados are in for a treat...a neo-pulp noir classic."

—*Chicago Tribune*

"No one can twist you through a maze with as much intensity and suspense as Max Allan Collins."

—*Clive Cussler*

"Collins never misses a beat...All the stand-up pleasures of dime-store pulp with a beguiling level of complexity."

—*Booklist*

"Collins has an outwardly artless style that conceals a great deal of art."

—*New York Times Book Review*

"Max Allan Collins is the closest thing we have to a 21st-century Mickey Spillane and...will please any fan of old-school, hardboiled crime fiction."

—*This Week*

"A suspenseful, wild night's ride [from] one of the finest writers of crime fiction that the U.S. has produced."

—*Book Reporter*

"This book is about as perfect a page turner as you'll find."

—*Library Journal*

"Bristling with suspense and sexuality, this book is a welcome addition to the Hard Case Crime library."

—*Publishers Weekly*

"A total delight...fast, surprising, and well-told."

—*Deadly Pleasures*

"Strong and compelling reading."

—*Ellery Queen's Mystery Magazine*

"Max Allan Collins [is] like no other writer."

—*Andrew Vachss*

"Collins breaks out a really good one, knocking over the hard-boiled competition (Parker and Leonard for sure, maybe even Puzo) with a one-two punch: a feisty story-line told bittersweet and wry...nice and taut...the book is unputdownable. Never done better."

—*Kirkus Reviews*

"Rippling with brutal violence and surprising sexuality...I savored every turn."

—*Bookgasm*

"Masterful."

—*Jeffery Deaver*

"Collins has a gift for creating low-life believable characters...a sharply focused action story that keeps the reader guessing till the slam-bang ending. A consummate thriller from one of the new masters of the genre."

—*Atlanta Journal Constitution*

"For fans of the hardboiled crime novel…this is powerful and highly enjoyable reading, fast moving and very, very tough."

—*Cleveland Plain Dealer*

"Entertaining…full of colorful characters…a stirring conclusion."

—*Detroit Free Press*

"Collins makes it sound as though it really happened."

—*New York Daily News*

"An exceptional storyteller."

—*San Diego Union Tribune*

"Nobody does it better than Max Allan Collins."

—*John Lutz*

And then, like punctuation to what I'd said, something landed heavily, thuddingly, out in the open area of the building, the central shaft area, a whump *sound with overtones of brittle breaking sounds, like a bag of laundry that had been heaved onto the cement, only somebody had left something breakable in some of the coat and pants pockets, something made of china perhaps, some things that would shatter when hitting the cement...*

I held Castile back with an arm, reached over with my free hand and flicked on a small lamp on an end table.

There was a naked body in the center of the floor, out in the open area. Oh, not exactly in the center, maybe, but close. The body was that of a man, and he'd hit face down, but twisting as he did, so that the trunk of him was visible, and there was no mistaking who it was...

HARD CASE CRIME BOOKS
BY MAX ALLAN COLLINS:

QUARRY
QUARRY'S LIST
QUARRY'S DEAL
QUARRY'S CUT
QUARRY'S VOTE
THE LAST QUARRY
THE FIRST QUARRY
QUARRY IN THE MIDDLE
QUARRY'S EX
THE WRONG QUARRY
QUARRY'S CHOICE
DEADLY BELOVED
SEDUCTION OF THE INNOCENT
TWO FOR THE MONEY
THE CONSUMMATA *(with Mickey Spillane)*

QUARRY'S CUT

by **Max Allan Collins**

A HARD CASE 

CRIME NOVEL

A HARD CASE CRIME BOOK
(HCC-S05)
First Hard Case Crime edition: October 2015

Published by

Titan Books
A division of Titan Publishing Group Ltd
144 Southwark Street
London SE1 0UP

in collaboration with Winterfall LLC

If you purchased this book without a cover, you should know that it is stolen property. It was reported as "unsold and destroyed" to the publisher, and neither the author nor the publisher has received any payment for this "stripped book."

Copyright © 1977 by Max Allan Collins.
Originally titled THE SLASHER.
Afterword © 2010, 2015 by Max Allan Collins.

Cover painting by Robert McGinnis

All rights reserved. No part of this book may be reproduced or transmitted in any form or by any electronic or mechanical means, including photocopying, recording or by any information storage and retrieval system, without the written permission of the publisher, except where permitted by law.

Print edition ISBN 978-1-78329-889-1
E-book ISBN 978-1-78329-890-7

Design direction by Max Phillips
www.maxphillips.net

Typeset by Swordsmith Productions

The name "Hard Case Crime" and the Hard Case Crime logo are trademarks of Winterfall LLC. Hard Case Crime books are selected and edited by Charles Ardai.

Printed in the United States of America

Visit us on the web at www.HardCaseCrime.com

This is for
Jay Lynch —
who advised against it

"I have a perfect cure for a sore throat—cut it."
ALFRED HITCHCOCK

"...[this is] one throat that deserves to be cut..."
JUDGE JOEL E. TYLER
ON FINDING *Deep Throat* OBSCENE

"I never did see one stag film where anybody got killed..."
LENNY BRUCE

QUARRY'S CUT

I

If it was Turner, I'd have to kill him.

Maybe it wasn't. I couldn't see the guy all that well, through the circle I made by rubbing my fist against the frosted-over windowpane. He was having gas put in his car, or rather was putting it in himself, at the self-service pump. A lanky, narrow-shouldered man with dark glasses and dark shaggy hair, wearing a green-and-brown plaid hunting jacket. Bending over, putting in gas...*if he turns and I get a better look...*

Only now the window was frosting up again. It was cold out there.

But warm enough in here, particularly if you'd had several bowls of Wilma's chili, which I had. Wilma was an enormously fat woman who liked her own cooking even better than those who made regular pilgrimages to her rambling two-story establishment, an oddball affair left over from some other decade, filling station, restaurant, grocery store and hotel all sharing the same slightly ramshackle roof.

Wilma came over and sat across from me in the booth, and I turned away from the window and marveled at her ability to squeeze her three or four hundred pounds in like that. She had curly brown hair and wore a red tent with yellow flowers on it. She was extraordinarily pretty, for a lady with half a dozen chins. She had the bluest eyes I ever saw on anybody who wasn't Paul Newman, including Robert Redford.

Business was good, for a couple weeks into April, with skiing season over and warm weather still a month away, easy. I took a lot of meals here, living only a quarter mile down the road, in an A-frame cottage on Paradise Lake; and during this past week I'd had Wilma's cooking pretty much to myself. But this was Friday and the weekend, and people drove over from Lake Geneva and everywhere else in the area to have a bowl of Wilma's chili, or some of her beer batter shrimp, or barbeque ribs, or any one of a dozen other items that were specialties of hers.

The room we were in was the tavern part, with a dining room off the rear. The room next door was the grocery store, among other things, all of the rooms having the same low ceiling and rough, gray wooden walls. It was one of those places that made no attempt to create an atmosphere and in so doing did.

"You're making money tonight, Wilma."

"Ain't shittin'," she said. She took some cigarettes out from somewhere in the flowered tent and didn't bother to offer me. She knew I didn't use them. She lit herself up and said, "See those crazy asses over there?"

She was pointing to a young couple in their early twenties, sitting in a booth across the room. I said I saw them.

"They drove down from Chicago for my chili. Can you beat it?"

I admitted I couldn't. "Who's helping you in the kitchen?"

"My niece. You saw her in here yesterday, didn't you? Little dark-haired girl with the titties?"

"That does sound familiar."

I rubbed the window again. Looked out. He wasn't there. Car was, though, a recent model Chevy, medium price range, blue-gray. He was probably paying for his gas.

"My father owned this place," she said.

Out of nowhere. She was like that, but this was something new, in subject matter. We'd become friends, over the several years I'd been living nearby, and spoke of many things, but never this.

"I never met your father," I said.

"I should hope to shout. He died in 1948."

"How old were you then?"

"None of your goddamn business. Twenty something. I did the cooking since I was thirteen."

"Who ran the place, after your father died?"

"I did. Who do you think? Took his name down and put mine up."

The painted sign outside said WILMA'S WELCOME INN.

"What about your mother?"

"She ran away with a vacuum cleaner man during the war."

"Which war?"

"I forget. You know, it's slow season and I got lots of empty rooms upstairs. Want to go up?"

"Not tonight. One of these days."

"Shit. I don't think you're ever gonna come across."

"It'll happen, Wilma. You can't rush love."

She liked that. She laughed about it. Her chins especially.

"Who's that guy out there, Wilma?"

"Who?"

I rubbed the frost off the window.

"The guy getting in his car," I said. "The guy getting in the Chevy. Ever seen him before, or is he just a tourist?"

"I seen him. Funny you should ask."

"Why's that?"

"He's got a room with me. Had it a week, now."

"So?"

"I think he banged my niece last night. I don't like that. She might've, but I don't. She's just sixteen and that fucker's forty."

"You want me to have a talk with him?"

"I could have Charley do that."

Charley was her bartender, a tough old bird in his early sixties.

"Let me," I said.

"You really want to?"

"I'd like to."

"Okay. He's in room twelve. But he's probably gone for the evening. He's gone most evenings till midnight."

"I'll just wait in his room and surprise him."

"You sure…"

"Sure."

"Okay, then. There's a master key on my office wall, on a nail."

I rubbed the window glass once again. Turner and his Chevy were gone.

I got up.

2

The last time I saw Turner was five years ago, and he was on the floor, where I put him, and he was telling me he'd fix me someday.

Childish, the way he put it really: "I'll fix you, fucker. I'll fix you."

And an hour or so earlier, we'd murdered a man. Or rather I had, with Turner giving me support, supposedly.

But it's necessary to go back before I first met Turner, before the Broker, even, if you're to understand any of this. It's necessary to go back as far as Vietnam, or at least to when I came home from Vietnam.

I found my wife in bed with a guy. It happens. It happens to a lot of people. Some of them maybe even take it well. I didn't. Not that I did anything rash. I just backed out of the room, apologizing, and returned the next day to the cozy clapboard in La Mirada where the guy, whose name was Williams, was in the driveway, under his sporty little car, the rear wheels jacked up, and he was so busy fixing the car he didn't have time for me, except to call me a bunghole, so I kicked the jack out.

It killed him. Not immediately, but soon. And my wife divorced me, and I couldn't have cared less, and lots of people were sympathetic—I wasn't even brought to trial over it—but a fuck of a lot of good it did me. My life was at a standstill—no wife, nobody else to speak of, no home, no work either. I was qualified to work as a garage mechanic, a skill I picked up as a kid, and also had a two-year degree from a junior college that should've paved the way for some kind of office work.

But the story had got some play in the papers, and adding that to the bad publicity Vietnam veterans were getting at the time anyway (we were all wild-eyed dopers, in case you forgot) prospective employers weren't exactly lining up to hire me.

Except for the Broker. He had work for me. He looked me up, a month or more after my marital difficulty hit the papers, found me in a hotel in L.A., a fleabag with hot and cold running whores, one of whom gave me a dose of something worse than anything you could catch in Nam, excluding a bullet of course. Earlier my old man had looked me up, came from Ohio to tell me not to come home. Said my stepmother had been uncomfortable around me even before I started killing people. I never did ask the old man which killing he meant: the one for revenge, or the dozen for democracy.

Which was part of what the Broker said to me that made so much sense, that night in my dreary paint-peeling hotel room, the glow of neon from outside providing the only light and giving everything a surreal look, including the Broker and his unlined face that could have belonged to a man of thirty, and his white hair/white mustache that could have belonged to a man of sixty. But even in the surreal glow he looked like the successful businessman he was, in his conservative yet stylish suit, and he talked like a politician, slick and eloquent and even seductive, and when he suggested I do in civilian life what I had done not so long ago as a soldier—that is, kill people—it seemed reasonable.

After all, I had killed people overseas for little money, and killed somebody since coming home for no money... why not do it for *real* money, for a change? And Broker was talking very real money—two thousand and up for a simple hit.

All of which stands as a gross simplification of what the Broker said to me. I have tried on several occasions to record the scene, but have always failed. I have good, almost uncanny recall; I've proven that, I think, in the three accounts I wrote previous to this one. But that first meeting with the Broker stays a blur in my mind; the sensations of it, the gist of what was said, that much I can tell you.

And I can tell you also I was an easy sale. Not that I was bloodthirsty or anything: I wasn't. I'm still not.

But he approached me at a time in my life when I could have gone in about any direction. I had nothing left but the contradictory notion that while life and death are meaningless, survival remains essential. It doesn't seem to make sense, I know, but it seemed to make sense in Vietnam, which is where I learned it. And it has stayed with me till this day.

The Broker was the middleman between client and

killer. He used to describe himself as "sort of an agent," and it's a good description of his role. A client would come to him with a problem, and the Broker would come to somebody like me to see to it a means was provided for solving that problem.

Actually, I was part of a team, a two-man team breaking down to active (hitman) and passive (back-up man). I usually played the former role, but not always. For most of the five years I worked through the Broker, I was teamed with a guy named Boyd, who has since been killed. But then so has the Broker.

The first year and a half or so, I filled in here and there, never working with a steady partner. Until Broker teamed me with Turner.

3

We did five jobs in six months, Turner and I, which is probably at least one too many. And maybe that had something to do with why Turner fucked up on number five. You can get sloppy, working too many jobs too close together. You can get careless. You can also get dead.

Which is why I resented what happened in Twin Cities, at the carnival.

It was the second week in June, cool, overcast, getting toward dusk; the carnival was on the fair grounds, which lay somewhat uneasily between Minneapolis and St. Paul, in the midst of residential and business areas. A big show, with a score of crazy rides: their bizarre, oversize metallic shapes—the Yo-Yo, the Loop, Zipper, Octopus, Tilt-a-Whirl, Doubledecker Ferris, Death-Wish Roller Coaster—rose out of the city of tents like lunatic skyscrapers. Along the wide, occasionally puke-strewn sawdust streets of this city, people strolled, particularly young people, sometimes couples, oftentimes packs of three or more of a single sex, middle-class kids in tight jeans and fresh faces, while skinny men with smoldering cigarettes behind ears and dark tee-shirts on and dark complexions or perhaps just in need of baths stood on platforms and spoke into loud, muffled mikes, extolling the desirability of viewing

In Person the Fattest Boy In The World, the Smallest Living Man In The World, the Strangest Teenage Women In The World (one of whom had no face, thanks to the radiation color TVs emit) and a woman who before your very eyes turned into a gorilla, and no doubt was the only one of her kind In The World, and other men, not all of them skinny in black tee-shirts but many of them needing baths, coaxed passersby into throwing balls and throwing money away (sometimes literally, in the dime/quarter/dollar toss) in pursuit of prizes of no discernible worth, including stuffed animals of indeterminate species and cigarette lighters with the American flag on them.

The mark was a guy running a game tent, a red canvas cubbyhole where you threw baseballs at milk bottles. You could win anything from a tiny stuffed skunk to a pink stuffed dog the size of a Volkswagen. Odds are you'd win the skunk.

The guy was short, fat and dark, Jewish maybe, or Italian. Could be either one, if he was a mob guy hiding out, which I figured him to be.

Understand, I was never told why this or any mark was getting hit, other than somebody wanted them hit bad enough to pay good money. Much of what I did for Broker was tied to the mob but only in that clients were often referred through mob sources; relatively little of what I or any of us did for Broker was directly Family-related. They had their own people to do that kind of thing, and only in special instances would it prove useful to them to bring in somebody outside, like me…

However, sometimes it was pretty obvious a hit was a

Family contract, and this time was one of them: the way the guy looked, not just his ethnic look but his vaguely urban speech and his almost polished manner—none of it fit the carny image. Not that everybody connected with the carnival was some kind of lowlife or deadbeat: not at all. But the professional carny men have a look to them, as does the summer help, the kids (including pretty college girls, some of whom work game tents, others of whom work as strippers) who do the carny number as a money-making lark. A guy like our short, fat, dark, somewhat well-bred mark sticks out like a nun at a nightclub.

I went over to his tent and threw some balls.

"Cool day," I said.

"Cool," he agreed. His voice was high-pitched, like it hadn't changed yet.

I seemed to be his first customer in some time, but he wasn't particularly excited about the prospect.

"How much?" I said, pointing to the pile of baseballs on the counter.

He pointed to the sign that said "3 Balls - 35¢, Everybody Wins." His features were bulges in his puffy face. His thinning gray-brown hair was cut short and neatly combed to the side. He was in his early fifties. He wore a Hawaiian print shirt and white pressed slacks. He looked like the host at a country club luau.

I threw three balls and won a skunk.

I threw three more and won another.

"What do I win," I asked, "if I play again and keep missing?"

"A skunk," he said.

"I figured. Well. Thanks."

"Don't mention it."

I walked away, passing several other game tents where the pitchmen did everything but reach out and grab me to pull me in for a game.

Shriners were standing around in their fezzes like foreign cops. Some of them were ticket-takers; others just stood and in so doing reminded anyone who cared that the Shrine was sponsoring all this family entertainment. One of the Shriners was Turner.

He was standing in a small open area between the House of Mirrors and the tent where the Bonnie and Clyde Death Car was being exhibited, and he was watching the pretty young girls in tight jeans go by. He was tall, a good three inches taller than my five ten, and while neither of us was overweight, he was leaner looking. His hair was dark brown and shaggy, his complexion pale, almost pasty, with heavy five o'clock shadow; his eyes were dark as his hair and so close-set they crowded his nose.

He nodded to me as I approached, saying, "How they hangin', Quarry?"

"Turner," I said, nodding back. We stood there a few minutes.

"Lots of nice pussy," he said, smirking. He did a lot of smirking. His voice was like sandpaper rubbing against itself.

I didn't say anything for a while.

"You won't see nicer pussy," he said. "Young pussy. Nice young pussy. You won't find pussy any tighter. You know what I'm talking about, Quarry?"

"It seems to have something to do with pussy."

"Bet your ass it does. You hungry?"

"I could eat."

So we went over to one of the few food stands that had a counter and stools, and ordered knockwurst sandwiches with grilled onions and peppers, and lemonade, and sat at the far end of the counter by ourselves and ate and talked.

"What do you think, Quarry? How's he look to you?"

"Like a bigger asshole than you."

"How'm I supposed to take that?"

"Any way you like."

"I don't get you, Quarry. Why the fuck you got to be so goddamn hard to get along with? I been trying to get along with you, you know."

"Sure."

"Well I am, goddamnit."

"Drop it, okay?"

This was only our second contact. Turner had been here a week, getting the mark's pattern down, and I got in last night. Today I was to see if the setup looked kosher enough to go ahead with the hit. We'd had words last night, at Turner's motel, about the way he was handling his end, his making like a Shriner as a cover. He thought it was a great idea. I thought it sucked. He could've picked up any number of menial jobs at the carnival that would've given him plenty of opportunity to stake out the mark; his acting the Shriner role was in my opinion idiotic, as the Shriners were local and could spot him as phony.

But the cover had held, apparently, probably because Turner had a good line of bullshit, so what the hell.

"I got to agree with you," Turner was saying, through a mouthful of knockwurst and onions and what have you, "the guy's an asshole. You'd think he'd have fucking sense enough to try and blend in. You'd think he'd notice all the noise the other pitchmen are making, and that he'd have sense enough to join in. But no. He just lays back quiet and waits for customers to come see him and when they do, he don't give a shit. He don't know much about being inconspicuous."

"Maybe you could give him some tips."

"What's that supposed to mean?"

"Guess."

"Hey, yeah, well and blow it out your ass, Quarry, if you want my opinion. So you going to tell me how it looks to you, or just sit there?"

"It looks okay."

"I think so, too. How's tomorrow afternoon sound?"

"Bad. They pull up stakes morning after next. Tomorrow being the last day might make it atypical. Since you went to the trouble of getting his pattern down, we ought to use it."

"I suppose. Fuck it, anyway."

"What's the problem?"

"I had a date tonight. This evening, I mean."

"A date."

"Yeah, I was going to get it on between shows with Zamorita."

"Zamorita."

"I been humping her. Zamorita. Actually, her name is Hilda something. She's the woman who turns into a gorilla."

"You have that effect on all the girls?"

"Funny. I mean, she's the one with the stage act. She gets in this cage and they dim the lights and do some electrical stuff and she turns into a gorilla. Anyway that's what it looks like. Actually it's just a big hoax."

"Oh, Turner, do you have to spoil everything?"

"You're a funny guy, Quarry. Funnier than my old man when he takes out his teeth. Anyway, I guess I'll just have to take a rain check on the bitch. Damn, is she going to be disappointed."

"I can imagine. Ten o'clock, then?"

"Ten o'clock. I'll be there."

"Where exactly?"

He pointed over to a spot near the mark's tent, between the exhibit with the giant rats and the House of Mirrors. The Winnebago camper was parked behind there, just fifty feet away, among many other such vehicles belonging to the carny people; in the background loomed the truck trailers the rides, when disassembled, were transported in.

"Okay," I said. "See you later."

"See you later."

I went on some rides, had my weight and age guessed and threw a few balls at a game tent, but not the mark's. I ended up in Fun World, a king-size arcade in a long, narrow tent. The pinballs and shooting machines held my attention for several hours, and when I finally came out, at nine-thirty, night had replaced dusk; the rides, with their bright neons of every imaginable color, were tracing garish designs against the darkness, like ungodly jewelry or a hand-painted tie.

And at nine-forty, after going to the rental Ford for my silenced nine-millimeter and a light jacket, I had wandered over by the mark's stall, where he was closing down. The rest of the carnival stayed open till one, but not this clown. He always closed up early, sometimes as early as ten o'clock. Tonight was a new record.

Which was a little disturbing. It's always disturbing when a mark varies his pattern, even just a little. But even more disturbing when I looked over where Turner was supposed to be and he wasn't. Well, it was early. He'd be along soon.

By nine fifty-five the mark's tent was shut down.

Still no Turner.

And the guy was heading back toward his Winnebago.

I hesitated.

Shit.

Turner would be here momentarily.

I went ahead and followed the guy to the camper. It was dark back there, and deserted, except for the mark and me. I took the silenced gun from out of my belt, where the light jacket had covered it, and went in right behind the guy, shutting the camper door behind us, flicking on the light and showing him the nine-millimeter.

And it should have been over just that fast. I should have squeezed the trigger, sent him on his way and me on mine.

But I was still pretty new at the game. I hadn't learned the desirability of doing it fast, not yet. In fact I was just in the process of learning.

Because in the split second I wasted, the fat little Jew or Italian or whatever the fuck he was reached over to the little built-in stove and got hold of a frying pan and laid it across the side of my face, and I fired but the silenced gun thudded a shot into the cushion of a chair, and there was grease in the pan, not hot thank God, but grease, and some of it got in my eyes and the little fucker had pushed me aside and was scrambling past me, out the door, before I could get my eyes working and my gun hand around to make up for my mistake.

I put the gun back in my belt. I had to: from the doorway of the camper I could see the mark heading into the carnival, that Hawaiian shirt flashing into the crowd, and I had to pursue him. And that could hardly be done with the nine-millimeter hanging out. I zipped the jacket up a third of the way and went after him.

One good thing, though: he'd angled toward the space of open ground between the giant rat exhibit and the House of Mirrors. Right into Turner's arms.

Only as I reached that point myself I saw the guy going into the House of Mirrors, nodding at the ticket-taker who knew him as a fellow carny and waved him by without a ticket.

And Turner was nowhere to be seen.

So I bought a ticket to the House of Mirrors.

It wasn't very busy right now, but I wouldn't be alone in there with him. I didn't know what compelled him to enter that place, but chances were he didn't know, either. It's easy to be critical of the behavior of people in tense situations: not everybody functions well under stress.

Or maybe he'd seen some movies with arty funhouse shootout scenes, and figured I'd be distracted by all those reflections of myself and he could maybe somehow lose me in there. Which was a possibility. Maybe it would have been smarter to just wait for him to come out.

But he might also know his way around in there; maybe he was a pretty good friend of the guy who ran the house, and knew where an office was or a back exit or something. Or maybe he figured he knew the place well enough to hide somewhere and jump me as I came by.

Who could tell what he thought.

At any rate, I found him, in an enclosed area of perhaps sixteen mirrors, none of them distorting, and nobody else was around at the moment, and if he thought hiding in the House of Mirrors would be to his advantage, he was wrong—unless he enjoyed watching all those images of himself getting shot through the sternum.

I found my way out with little trouble. Behind me I heard somebody finding him, and making a fuss, going into a screaming panic. That was too bad. Had everything gone as it should, the mark would have been found no sooner than morning, in all probability.

I found Turner in the trailer behind the Gorilla Girl's tent.

I knocked and, finally, was answered by a pretty brunette of about twenty, though her face was an easy ten years harder.

"Tell Cheetah Tarzan's here to see him," I said.

"Go away," she said, starting to push shut the door.

I pushed it open and found Turner naked in bed and pulled him out by the arm and threw him on the floor.

"What the hell…?" he said.

I kicked his balls up in him.

That kept him busy for a few minutes, during which time I told Zamorita to get him his clothes.

"I'll fix you, fucker," he said, after a while, still holding himself. "I'll fix you."

"Never mind that," I said. "You better just get your pants on so we can both get the hell out of here."

Now, five years later, going through Turner's room at Wilma's Welcome Inn, I wondered why I bothered going back for him at all.

4

From the window above the old-fashioned radiator in Turner's room I could see my A-frame cottage clearly, despite the partial sheltering of trees. The radiator was hot and making hissing noises, complaining about its unexpected April workload; but at least it helped keep the frost off the window, which was a plus for Turner, as he was apparently using this window to watch me, to study my pattern. He no doubt used the same binoculars I was now using: I'd found them in his bottom dresser drawer, between a box of .380 shells and the Browning they were used in.

A gunsmith had done some improvising on the automatic, because the original barrel was gone and replaced with a new one that had a built-in silencer. I didn't see the point, as the length of the new barrel was practically the same as the old one would've been with silencer attached. So nothing in particular had been gained, and something had been lost: the ability to detach the silencer, which is nice to be able to do at times, as they aren't always necessary and do make the weapon more bulky. But to each his own.

The room was orderly, though Wilma did not provide maid service. That is, unless the sixteen-year-old niece

Turner was humping was playing housekeeper, too. There was just the one big room, with a double bed with maple headboard against the left side wall, and a living-room area opposite, with sagging couch and a chair or two and a beat-up coffee table with a scuffed metallic portable TV on it. The wallpaper was flowered and purple-faded-to-gray. Varnished light wood floors showed around the worn edges of the large round braided rug. There was no john (other than the floor's communal one, down the hall) and a single, shallow closet he hadn't hung anything in was behind the couch, in the corner. The dresser was over left of the window, near the bed; its drawers contained clothing and what I mentioned before. His shaving kit was on top of the dresser, which had a mirror. On the floor under the bed was a stack of skin magazines, of which *Hustler* was the most genteel.

I was surprised I could find nothing in writing, no record of my activities as noted by Turner. He might possibly be keeping that on his person, in a little notebook or something, but I didn't think it likely: the kind of record a person working stakeout would keep isn't easily kept in anything smaller than a secretarial-size pad, and Turner's habit during the time he'd worked backup for me had been to use a spiral notebook larger than that. Of course that was five years ago.

Which in itself had me thinking. It was a little late in the day for Turner to come looking for revenge. Five years ago I'd kicked him in the balls, and reported him fucking up to the Broker, but it hadn't cost Turner anything:

Broker had simply put him with another partner. I didn't doubt Turner carried a grudge against me, but I did doubt it was big enough a one for him to come looking for me with a gun.

Besides, he was obviously on stakeout duty. Which meant he was part of a team, and not the trigger part, either. He was hired help and nothing more. My first instinct was to tie his presence here in with the bad blood between us: but I no longer felt that way. Turner was not working on his own initiative.

So I'd just have to talk to him and find out who hired him. Or at least find out who his new Broker was, so I could put a gun to that guy's head and get the name of whoever it was took the contract out.

I put the binoculars in the dresser, but stuck the Browning in my belt. I turned out the lights and went over to the couch to wait for Turner to come.

I didn't let myself think. There was a lot to think about, a lot in my life that was threatened by all of this, not the least of which was my life itself, but I didn't think. I didn't let myself. There are times when it's smart to sort through the things that have been happening to you, and figure out what it is they all mean, and there are times to clear all the shit out of your head, empty your head of everything but *now*, so you are ready, not edgy, but on edge, perched like an animal waiting for its prey to make a move. So I sat on the uncomfortable, spring-bulging couch, waiting for Turner to come.

In two hours and some odd minutes, I heard his voice.

It was still grating, had that same sandpaper quality. He was standing outside his door, talking to somebody. And that could be a problem.

The other person spoke, and it was a girl, a young woman's voice. Possibly the sixteen-year-old niece Wilma was worried about.

A key was working in the door, in the lock, and I ducked into the closet, to the rear of the couch.

"Don't worry, baby," he was saying. I heard the door close. I heard a thud, which I guessed to be the sound of his hunting jacket being tossed on the couch. "She works till two in the morning. It ain't even midnight. We got plenty of time."

"If she finds us together," the girl said, her voice sounding very young, "she'll kill us."

"Aw the hell with her. You going to let some fat old windbag run your life?"

"She's my aunt."

"She can't give you this."

There followed considerable moaning and groaning, most of it from the girl. In the background the radiator hissed.

"Here. Let me help you out of that stuff."

"No...I'll...I'll do it."

I was sitting on the floor. It was cramped in there. I decided I might as well enjoy myself, so I looked through the keyhole while the girl undressed. My view was partially blocked by the couch, but I saw everything, as the girl moved around a little, placing her clothing piece by piece over on the dresser.

She was small, tan and big-breasted, with a simple, pretty face that had those same blue eyes as fat Wilma. She had shoulder-length dark brown hair and an equally dark brown pubic tangle that started as a trail at her navel and turned into a dense undergrowth soon after; it was a place you could get lost in for weeks. I hoped her overage boyfriend wouldn't be quite that long.

Turner took his clothes off, then. That I didn't bother watching. I felt stupid, like a husband who didn't have it right: the idiot didn't realize it was the *lover* who hid in the closet, not the cuckold.

Then the bed was making noise and so were they. The radiator got its two cents in, too.

Me, I was slouched quietly down in the closet, back to the wall, gun in my lap.

Still waiting for Turner to come.

5

He and the girl stayed in the sack nearly two hours. I didn't watch much of it, though the keyhole provided an unexpurgated if small-screen view of the proceedings. Between rounds he would teach the girl things to do to him, and watching her crawl around on the bed and him doing them certainly beat watching reruns of *Celebrity Bowling*. But eventually, inevitably, he'd get on top of her and stay on top, which meant the view I had was largely of him, and I wasn't particularly interested in looking up that asshole's asshole.

So I sat there, patiently, my state of mind remarkably serene for a guy hiding in a closet, and why not. Turner was in a tighter box than I was, and I don't mean that in the sense of a pun. He was in a very bad situation and didn't know it, which was part of what made it so bad.

I admit he was having a better time than I was, but that was largely because he was a man who thought he had a gun in a nearby dresser drawer and didn't know that gun was still nearby but now in the possession of somebody in a closet a few feet away, waiting to possibly put that gun to use. Ignorance is bliss, all right, but it's also a good way to get blown away. And that's no pun, either.

The only reason I was sitting this out, of course, was the girl. Turner alone I could handle, no problem—or anyway not much of one. Turner in the company of an innocent third party was something else again. Particularly when that innocent third party was Wilma's niece, whose honor I was here on the pretense of defending, even though from my occasional glimpses through the keyhole I could see there wasn't much left to defend.

Contrary to what you might think, assuming you've read some of the bullshit fiction books written on people like me, or seen some of the ridiculous movies or TV things done on us, a paid killer is not usually a person who will be careless about killing, who would go out casually, heedlessly mowing down anyone who crossed his path in the course of a job. The killing of one person, if it's handled with some intelligence and care, generally causes little commotion, unless the town is exceptionally small, or the mark exceptionally well known. A murder is likely to be buried in the back of the papers the day it happens, in a major city, and on the front page and on TV for a day or so in a secondary-size city, and in either case consigned to the unsolved file of the cops after a few weeks of fruitless investigation.

But kill two people and the shit will hit the fan. Kill an innocent bystander, indiscriminately, without the planning that went into hitting the mark, and suddenly it's on TV constantly and in the papers continuously and everybody's hollering "Mass murder!" and the cops will have to go after it for however long it takes, because the media and the media-manipulated public will demand nothing less.

Even had I been on a job, out in the field somewhere, keeping all this in mind would have been necessary, important; here, at home, in my literal back yard, it was an overriding concern. Contact with Turner that involved Wilma's niece would be unfortunate, even if the girl didn't get killed.

So I sat, and I waited, and my back started hurting and the sweat started to roll down my face and everywhere else, because it was hot in there and stuffy, the air as stale as a political speech, and then I noticed them talking. Their voices were taking on a tone of normalcy, as opposed to the assorted sounds of sexual craziness that had been playing in the background during my confinement, like a pervert's substitute for Muzak.

"It's ten till two," the girl was saying.

"Maybe you better go, then," Turner said.

Who said chivalry was dead.

"I know, but…I don't want to go. I want to stay with you. All night."

"Nice if you could. But if you think you should go, you better."

"I guess I better."

"Here, I'll help you get dressed."

He had her dressed and out the door in three minutes; the poor little bitch had to ask for her goodnight kiss.

And then he stood in the middle of the room, right in my line of vision, stood naked, his sex shrunken like he'd just come out from swimming in very cold water, which wasn't exactly the case, and he looked at the door the girl had just exited through and said, "Hee hee," several times, and slapped his belly, as it wasn't every day Turner got to diddle a sixteen-year-old. He scratched his sides and yawned and left my line of vision long enough to switch off the lights and then a few seconds later I heard him crawl into bed.

Pretty soon he starting snoring, and that's when I got to my feet, ducking the metal pipe that cut across the closet, the empty hangers presenting a danger, if I bumped into them and rattled them together. But I didn't, and the closet door eased open soundlessly and none of my bones creaked either, despite the cramped position they'd been in for two hours, and I started across the room.

Some moonlight was filtering through the trees and in the window, bathing the room in semi-visibility. He was sleeping on his back, naked, on top of the blankets, possibly because the room was nice and warm from the radiator, or maybe he was still aglow from fucking his teenager.

Sometimes I think stupidity is contagious. I was so used to Turner doing dumbass things that I forgot he was a professional. An asshole, an idiot, but a professional. Which meant don't underestimate him. Which meant you had to expect anything could happen. You had to be ready for a snoring man to suddenly whip an arm out at you and knock you over against the wall, and then come diving toward you like a linebacker going for the quarterback.

He buried his head in my chest and pinned me to the wall and threw some punches into my ribs and stomach and I batted him alongside his head with the Browning, caught some ear and got some blood going, and he stopped pummeling for a second and in that second must've realized I had his gun, or anyway *a* gun, and both his hands went for my gun arm, one hand around my wrist, the other catching me between shoulder and arm, his nails long and cutting the flesh of my wrist, a thumb digging up under into my armpit, and with his two hands he tried for a while to see if he couldn't convince my right arm to abandon my body.

But I still had a left hand, and with it I grabbed a handful of wilted, exposed balls and squeezed and squeezed some more and twisted too and he released his grip on my arm and opened his mouth to scream but I put him to sleep with another whap on the head with the Browning before the scream got going.

He wasn't out long. He would've been, maybe, if I hadn't kicked him awake when he started in snoring again.

He looked up at me, hands cupping himself, squinting up in the half-darkness, and said, "Jesus…it's Quarry."

"I thought maybe you'd recognize me," I said.

6

I told him to go sit on the couch and he did. I turned on the lights and he asked me if he could put something on. I said no. I said I had something in common with his girlfriends: I liked him better naked.

Actually, he wasn't much to look at, no matter what sex you were. He was just a narrow-shouldered, skinny man, though he had a spare tire he was working on, and his thick, shaggy head of hair was like a fright wig, his flesh pasty white with occasional dark body hair, and his Nixon-like five o'clock shadow. He looked very worried, and confused, sitting there slump-shouldered, looking up at me like a kid worried about getting grounded by a particularly strict old man.

He waited a long time for me to talk. When I didn't, he said, "I…I don't understand, Quarry. What are you doing here? What's this all about?"

I went over by the window, leaned against the ledge in front of it, the Browning at my side. I looked out the window, toward my cottage.

"Quarry? Why don't you say something?"

"Why don't you?"

"What the fuck you think I been doing?"

"Stalling. Playacting. Something."

"Nothing. Nothing like that. I honest to Christ don't know what this is about. Is it..."

"Is it what?"

"A contract? Somebody took a contract out on me? And...you're here to fill it? Is...is that it?"

I said nothing.

"Who'd want to kill me? I don't have an enemy in the world."

"How about that sixteen-year-old's aunt?"

"What's the game, Quarry? I'm not actually supposed to believe you're morally outraged by me humping some little piece of jailbait, am I?"

"Am I here making a citizen's arrest, you mean? No."

"Then...why...what...?"

I said nothing.

"Jesus, Quarry. I...I mean. I haven't thought of you in years. I haven't seen you since that carnival thing."

I said nothing.

"Are you listening to what I'm saying, Quarry? I am saying I honest to Christ don't know what this is about. I don't see you in five years and you show up in my hotel room and tear my fucking nuts half off, Jesus. It's crazy. You're crazy."

"What are you doing here, Turner?"

"What do you mean?"

I said nothing.

"I'm here on business."

"On what?"

"Business. I'm here on a job."

"What sort of job."

"Same. Same as when you and me worked together. What about you, Quarry? I heard you left the business."

"And here I thought you hadn't heard about me in five years."

"I didn't say that, exactly. I did hear about you."

"Who from?"

"Guy I work with."

"Name of?"

"Burden."

"Don't think I know him."

"Short guy, balding, on the heavy side. In his late forties, early fifties."

"Don't know him."

"He doesn't know you, either."

"He just tells people about me."

"We were talking one time, we were talking about people we worked with. Your name come up. He heard about you from some other guy he worked with."

"Name of?"

"Ash."

"Ash I know."

"Sure. You worked with Ash, right after Broker split you and me up, right?"

"That's right."

"It's funny, what happened with the Broker, isn't it."

"A stitch."

"I mean…I heard you was there."

"I was."

"Did you, uh, kill him or what?"

"Why not ask Burden?"

"I already did. He said Ash said maybe you killed Broker, maybe not. Probably not, he said."

"I was there when Broker bought it."

"You were there."

"I didn't pull the trigger."

"Oh. Who did? Anybody I know?"

"Kid named Carl. Bodyguard of Broker's."

"Don't know him."

"You won't get the pleasure. Him I did kill."

"Oh. Well. What line you in these days, anyway?"

"I'm the house dick here."

"Funny. You're still funny as a crutch, Quarry."

"Well I'm not naked and stupid, which I admit makes it tougher to get the laughs. But then I have the gun. So I get to ask the questions, now that the small talk is out of the way. Once again. Why are you here?"

"On a job, I said."

"Tell me about the mark."

"The mark?"

"It's a term meaning the poor son of a bitch you're here to help snuff."

"You don't want to know about that."

"I don't."

"You know you don't. You know that's something I can't tell you. You know that better than me, that somebody in our line don't go around spreading the mark's name around."

"Somebody in our line doesn't fuck teenagers when he's out on a job, when he's supposed to be inconspicuously getting his work done."

"Where do you think I was tonight for three hours? I was working."

"Be more specific."

"Quarry, be reasonable!"

"The mark, Turner. Tell me about him. Or her."

"Him."

"Okay. Him."

"I can't tell you."

"Then I'll ask the inside of your head, after it slides down the wall behind you."

"You wouldn't do that. You're too careful for that kind of thing, Quarry. You don't go around killing people without..."

"You have five seconds."

"Bullshit."

"One."

"His name is Castile."

"As in Spain."

"Yeah. As in Spain. As in *Captain from Castile.* That's an old movie you may have seen."

"I've seen it. Tyrone Power's in it. He's dead. In a few seconds you can ask him what *he* thought of the film."

"What, do you think I'm stalling?"

"Two."

"Anyway, his name is Jerry Castile."

"I heard that name some place."

"Probably have. He makes movies."

"What kind of movies?"

"The kind you're thinking. Porno."

"Go on."

"He's up here working on a film. A porno flick."

"And?"

"And he's here with some people who are staying at this ski lodge or hunting lodge or something. It's off in the boonies."

"How far off?"

"Just a few miles from here, actually. But it's off the main roads. Back deep in a wooded place. They're all staying there, cast and crew and everybody. At first they weren't. They were at the Playboy Club, at Lake Geneva, that hotel or whatever the fuck over there. That was a week ago. Last five days they been at this lodge."

"And the mark is Jerry Castile."

"That's right."

"That's not a bad story. Try again."

"Try again? Quarry, you crazy fucker…you wave that goddamn Browning at me all night and count to five and count to five hundred and I won't be able to give you any other story, except a lie, Quarry, and what good would that do you?"

The hell of it was I believed him. He simply wasn't that good an actor, not that good a liar, either, to bluff this way, so thoroughly and so well. I'd been standing by the window, looking now and then toward my A-frame, and not a flicker, not a thing was going on in Turner's face by way of reaction, and while his life depended on the quality of his acting, I knew from past experience he wasn't up to this kind of performance. Unless he'd improved a hell of a lot in five years…

"I suppose you have notes," I said.

"Little notebook in my jacket pocket," he said.

The jacket was on the couch, nearby.

"Get it out."

"Really?"

"Go ahead and get it."

"I mean…aren't you a little leery about me trying something?"

"Not at all. I'd like it."

"I think maybe you would, Quarry. Here it is. Should I toss it?"

"No," I said, and came and got it. I flipped through it, one-handed; the notes were sparse and not particularly thorough, making use of a number system I didn't quite follow, though it obviously recorded the times of activities carried out by somebody. "I don't see the name of Castile, anywhere."

"It's there. In code."

"Code."

"Yeah. He's in there as ten dash three."

I looked and saw "10-3" throughout.

"Any special reason for choosing that?"

"J is the tenth letter of the alphabet, C is the third. J.C. Jerry Castile."

"Or Jesus Christ."

"Ain't you heard, Quarry? That sucker's already dead."

"Yeah, him and Tyrone Power both. It's a goddamn epidemic. That's some code. It'd probably take a Boy Scout a good two minutes to crack."

"I had to explain it to you, didn't I?"

"Well that's true. You have me there. But I seem to have you."

"What are you going to do with me?"

"That's a problem."

"Why?"

"Because I think I maybe believe you."

"About Castile, you mean? Of course you believe me. I'm telling you the truth."

"Maybe. Maybe."

"So what happens now?"

"I'm going to knock you out."

"Do you have to?"

"You're going to wake up again. What more do you want?"

"I want to reverse this situation sometime."

"Maybe you will. Do me one favor."

"What?"

"Don't mess around with that little girl anymore."

"Why? What's it to you?"

"Boring."

And I hit him with his Browning, and left the gun in his lap, empty, the clip in my pocket, but the box of slugs still in the dresser.

7

Wilma was waiting downstairs, at the bar. She looked especially big, poised on the barstool like a magician's balancing act. She also looked tired and not a little old, the oddly pretty blue eyes barely visible under heavy lids, the rows of chins hanging limp and loose, a cigarette drooping from her mouth like another tired appendage. The bartender, Charley, was putting glasses away nearby. He was bald and friendly looking but a hard-ass old guy who was also bouncer for the place. He and Wilma apparently had a thing, though nothing was ever said about it.

"About gave up on you," Wilma said.

"I talked to him," I said, taking a stool.

"And?"

"He'll stay away from her."

"I think the son of a bitch was with her tonight."

"I know he was. But I think it'll be the last night."

"Well. I owe you."

"No you don't."

"Shit if I don't. Have Charley pour you one."

"No thanks. I'd take coffee, though."

"Sure. Charley?"

He went after some coffee.

"I do appreciate what you done. That peckerhead

looked shifty to me, forty or better and her only sixteen, Jesus."

"The guy *is* shifty. Does he stay in his room most of the time?"

"Not really. Comes and goes. Why?"

"Oh, I don't know, Wilma. Just curious."

"Think he might be up to something on the shady side?"

"Could be. I don't know."

Charley came with a pot of coffee and poured Wilma and me a cup, and went back to wiping the glasses. He hovered nearby, listening, but not participating.

"Let me give you some advice, Wilma."

"Sure."

"Stay away from the guy. I got him straightened out, I think. But at the same time keep an eye on him. And if he messes around with your niece anymore, you can let me know and I'll talk to him again."

"You really think he's some kind of crook or something, is that it?"

"No, no. But keep your distance from him."

"And my eyes open?"

"That'd be smart, I think."

"Okay."

"Thanks for the coffee."

"Stop by for lunch tomorrow. It'll be on the house."

"I just might take you up on that."

"You better."

"Goodnight, Wilma. Charley."

And I went home.

8

I went home and considered the things Turner had told me.

And the more I considered them, the more likely it seemed they were true. I began to believe that Turner really was here on a job, to help rid the world of some porno movie mogul, that Turner's presence here, a literal stone's throw from my door, was sheer coincidence.

But sheer coincidences are something I have always had trouble swallowing. This one was no exception. In my line of work, it pays to be skeptical, even paranoid, especially in the face of anything even vaguely coincidental. Otherwise you may find yourself dead. And death is nature's way of telling you you fucked up.

Still, there was reason to believe Turner, and not just because of his convincing performance: Wilma's description of Turner coming and going did not fit the pattern of a guy doing stakeout duty. That supported the notion that the mark was someone other than me.

I was considering all of this while sitting on the couch in the open loft that looks out on the living room of my A-frame cottage. Downstairs, under the loft, were two more bedrooms, a laundry room and a john. A kitchenette was off to one side of the living room. A modest, comfortable little place, with a beautiful lake at the edge of the front yard. It was a home, a life, worth fighting to keep.

I was sitting with my nine-millimeter in my hand. The silencer was on. There was, I thought, at least some chance of my having to use the gun sometime tonight.

If Turner had lied to me, if the real reason he was staying at Wilma's Welcome Inn was to watch me and set me up for the kill, he and/or his partner would make their attempt tonight, or not at all. Possibly not at all, since I had seen him and talked to him and would be expecting him. And if they didn't try tonight, the hit would be scratched and they would have to go back to the middleman who gave them the assignment and say that the mark (me) had made Turner, so the game was off. And the middleman would send somebody else, later, to try again.

If the hit was scratched, Turner would of course expect me to try to follow him home. But I wouldn't need to do that. I could wait a week or so and then pull Turner's card from the Broker's file and go to Turner's home base and stake him out and wait for him to lead me to whoever his middleman was. From the middleman I could find out who took the contract out on me and do something about it.

Turner didn't know about the Broker's file. It included fifty names, fifty entries, with extensive biographical information, current and past addresses, photos and a listing of specific jobs carried out. The fifty people in Broker's file were the people who used to work through him. People like me. Like Turner. Killers for hire.

I'd inherited the file, indirectly, after Broker was killed, earlier that year. I have recorded all of that in some detail, elsewhere, and won't go into it again here.

But I should explain what the file had come to mean in my life. The years of working through a middleman—a Broker—had ended in a series of doublecrosses that convinced me I would never put up with such an arrangement again, that I would work for myself, and only myself: my life in *my* hands…not the Broker's.

So I devised a way of making that file of Broker's work for me. I would choose a name from it—the name of someone else like myself, who murdered for hire, by contract—and I would go stake out that someone, follow him to his latest assignment, and, once having determined who his potential target was, I would approach said target and offer my services.

That was the tricky part: approaching someone and saying, "Somebody's been hired to kill you." But such people tend to lead the sort of lives that include the possibility of violence, or they wouldn't be on the receiving end of a contract: nice, quiet, respectable people seldom are assassinated. The potential targets also tend to be the sort of people who like my solution to their problem: that is, killing the killers, and also finding out (and presumably taking care of) whoever hired the killers.

All of which is not entirely relevant to the story at hand, but it is hard for me to explain my state of mind, where Turner was concerned, without discussing the file. Because it seemed to me possible that someone had found out—or figured out—that I had the Broker's file; I had made an effort to lead the Broker's associates to believe that the file was destroyed, but perhaps that effort had been less successful than I thought. If someone knew I had the Broker's file, that, in itself, was good enough reason for Turner being sent to kill me.

Anyway, for now there was nothing to do but sit with gun in hand and wait and see if Turner was going to try and kill me. If he blew up my house or set fire to it or something, he could possibly get the job done, even now. Only he wasn't imaginative or bold enough for anything like that. He'd come plodding in, about half an hour before dawn, probably, and I'd kill him, after getting the name of his new Broker out of him. Or maybe he'd come with his partner. Burden, wasn't that the name he'd used? In which case I'd kill them both. But Jesus I hated the idea of that happening here, at home. It could be a messy, unpleasant business.

But maybe Turner had been telling the truth....

I waited.

It was a long night. I drank coffee. Lots of it. I read a paperback western and when my eyes got heavy, I allowed myself the television, playing the volume so low by morning I had perfected my lip reading.

He didn't come. Not him or his partner, not anybody, and I waited until noon, when I decided to take Wilma up on that free lunch.

The cottage had been warm and the air a little stale, so the outside air, which was cold and a slap in the face, was okay with me. I felt almost refreshed, nearly awake, by the time I'd walked the short distance to Wilma's Welcome Inn, and you'd never guess I had been up so long.

There was a "Closed" sign in the window, but the door was unlocked, so I went on in. Charley was alone in the tavern area, sitting in a booth, with his hands folded.

"Where's Wilma?" I said "What's going on?"

"She's at Johnson's," he said. His voice was strange, strained.

"Johnson's? What's that?"

"A funeral home."

"Who died?"

"She did."

9

Charley said it was okay if I had a look around. I saw the stairs, where she had fallen, a steep but tightly enclosed flight of stairs, with a rail, and between the rail and the close walls, you'd think a big woman like Wilma would've been able to catch herself, to brace her fall at least a little bit. But she hadn't. She'd fallen the entire flight and by the time she landed, her neck was broken and her life over.

No one had seen it happen. No one had even heard it. There was only one person staying in the hotel section of Wilma's Welcome Inn, a man registered as Paul Thomas, and he had apparently packed up and left early that morning, before the accident, Charley said. During the slow season, Wilma didn't open up till midmorning, ten o'clock, and that was only the grocery store section: the restaurant didn't open until eleven-thirty, for lunch. The stairs were in the grocery section, in the rear, near a check-in desk that was usually unmanned this time of year. It was somewhat unusual for even Wilma herself to be in the place before nine-thirty; she didn't live on the premises, but across the street in a two-story white clapboard. That's where Charley lived, too, though this was the first I'd heard him actually admit it, even if it was common knowledge around here. He said he woke up and Wilma was gone; he supposed she'd decided to come over early and do some cleaning. Sometimes she'd go over about an hour early and do that. This time, while in the process of doing her cleaning, she had apparently stumbled and fallen down the steps. Apparently.

At any rate, it had obviously happened before ten-thirty, which was when Charley came across the street to work, and found her.

I climbed the stairs and walked down the narrow hall to the room Paul Thomas, that is, Turner, had so recently vacated. He hadn't even shut the door, he'd gone out so fast. The drawers he'd emptied to fill his suitcase hung open like tongues sticking out at me. I went over the room carefully, to see if he'd left anything behind in his haste, and he had. Under the bed, was his stack of girlie magazines. I took them with me.

I stood and looked down the stairwell. Looked at the railing, at those narrow walls. There was only one way Wilma could've fallen here and died, and that was if she were unconscious before she started her fall.

I rejoined Charley, who was still sitting in the booth, with his hands folded.

"Who came around?" I asked him.

"I don't know exactly. I called Sam Keenan and he took care of all of it."

Keenan was a semi-retired doctor in his early sixties, from Chicago, who now lived in a cottage near mine, year-round.

"The ambulance was from Johnson's Funeral Home, over in Geneva, and I let them have her. There were some people from the Sheriff's department, too. I guess Sam called them. I didn't."

"What did the Sheriff's people have to say?"

"Not much. They asked some questions, quite a few, actually. Looked over where it happened pretty close. They just left, not five minutes before you came in the door."

"Do they suspect foul play?"

"Foul play?" He was genuinely surprised, looking up from his folded hands like he was noticing for the first time I was here. "What are you talking about?"

"I just wondered."

"Why?"

"Oh, seemed a little unlikely she'd fall and not catch herself, is all."

"She was a big woman…a big, fat woman. She was clumsy sometimes, like a fat woman will be. That's really all she was, a big fat woman." He was talking through his teeth. His fists were clenched. His eyes weren't wet, but they weren't right, either.

"I'm sorry about this, Charley."

"I did time."

"What?"

"I did time. They might suspect foul play, at that. You might be right. She knew I did time. She knew I stole, she knew when she hired me. She didn't give a shit. She trusted me, put me in charge of all her money. She didn't care, but they will. Can you picture it? They'll see she left the place to me. She told me that, she told me she had a will made and that I was to get this place if something happened to her. So now they'll see that and see about me doing time in Joliet…liquor store I robbed, about fifteen years ago…and they'll think maybe I killed her. And that kills me. The thought that anybody could think I'd kill her, harm her in any way, it fucking kills me."

"I wouldn't worry about that, Charley."

"Who's worried? I'm not worried. I don't give a shit. What can they do to me? She's dead."

"I'm afraid so."

"I wish somebody had killed her."

"What?"

"I wish somebody had killed her. I wish it hadn't been an accident. Then I could put the fucker that did it between my hands and squeeze the life out of him like pus out of a boil, and maybe some of the pus that's building up in me would get squeezed out, too. But I can't do that. Instead, she's just dead and there's not a goddamn thing I can do about it."

"Charley, is that niece of Wilma's around? I'd like to talk to her."

"She's over at the house. Across the street. She was with me when I found the body. Took it pretty hard. Why do you want to talk to her?"

"Just want to express my sympathy."

10

The house sat on a big open yard, a few pathetic bushes clustered around the front steps, but that was all; no trees were anywhere in sight, except way off in the back, in some other yard. It was a vacant lot with a house on it, plopped down there by an Oz-like wind, maybe, a two-story white clapboard with a front porch with a swing and if you looked close enough you might find Norman Rockwell's signature in the corner. The girl was sitting on the swing. She was not swinging. Not today, anyway.

The porch was not enclosed so I could walk up the steps and sit across from her on the ledge of the porch without seeming a total intruder.

"I don't think I know your name," the girl said. Her voice was young-sounding. It had sounded young last night, too. But even younger now.

"I don't know yours, either," I admitted.

"But you know who I am."

"Yes. Do you know who I am?"

"A customer at my aunt's."

"Yes."

"More than that, really. She liked you. She always smiled real big when she saw you coming."

"She smiled at everybody."

"I guess so. At some people especially. One time after you were in for supper and left, she said something about how quiet you were and that you weren't as tough as you think you are."

"I don't think I'm tough."

"I wouldn't know. It's just something I overheard."

I'd overheard some things last night myself; I felt a little uncomfortable in my private knowledge, of my having been an unseen spectator last night, during her fun and games with Turner or Thomas or whatever he might call himself. An asshole by any other name…

She was sitting in a shadow and her features were indistinct. Then I realized I was providing the shadow, and moved, and got a better look at her. She was still small and tan, with a lot of dark hair falling down behind her shoulders, pulled away from a pretty if not striking face that looked thirteen and thirty. Her eyes, I remembered, were Wilma's: her eyes, today, were haunted. She was wearing a sweatshirt that said MARY HARTMAN, MARY HARTMAN on it, and jeans; both were baggy and obscured the mature figure I'd seen through the keyhole.

"Are you here for a reason?"

"I'm sorry about your aunt."

"I know. Thank you for taking time to say so."

I said nothing.

"Please. I don't mean to be rude, but could you go, now? I'd like to sit here alone and just be kind of quiet for a while."

"I don't mean to be rude, either, but I need to ask you some questions."

"I don't understand."

"I know about your friend. Mr. Thomas. Room twelve?"

Her face went pale, or tried to, under the tan. She rose and said, "I'm going in the house, now."

"I'm coming with you."

"No…"

"Then sit back down on the swing."

"I won't…"

"I talked to him last night. Your aunt asked me to. To tell him to lay off you."

"She did. And what did he say?"

"He said you had the hairiest tight little pussy he ever dove into."

Her mouth fell open in a kind of horror and she covered it with one cupping hand and sat back down on the swing and began to weep, convulsively.

It wasn't a nice thing to say, and was of course a lie; but it got her attention.

"He isn't a nice man, your Mr. Thomas."

"Neither…neither…neither are you."

"That's true. But I'm not here to fuck you."

"Do you…have to use language like that?"

"I know some of my words aren't pretty. Neither is the world, sometimes. Neither was the sight of your aunt at the bottom of those steps with her neck broken, I'd imagine."

"Oh, please…please stop."

I sat on the swing by her. I reached out to touch her

shoulder, then thought better of it. I tried to put the intent of that gesture into the sound of my voice.

"I want you to tell me what happened this morning," I said. "Something happened between you, your aunt and Mr. Thomas. Tell me what it is."

She looked at me with big, beautiful wet blue eyes. They grabbed at me somewhere, in the back of my throat or in my stomach or somewhere, where I didn't know I could be reached anymore, and held me and I had this crazy urge to reach out to her, to hold her, and not for any reason remotely sexual, but then the urge passed, and I was glad it did.

"How did you know?" she said.

"I didn't," I said. "Not for sure. Until you confirmed it just now."

"Please…please don't play any more of these games with me."

"No games. I had a good idea something happened. It might have happened just between your aunt and Mr. Thomas, without you around. But when I saw you, here, on the swing, I could tell. I could tell you were there."

"I wasn't there when it happened. I didn't know my aunt had…fallen…until I saw her, when Charley and I, we found her, this morning. But I was there, earlier, when…" And she shuddered.

"Go on."

"I got up this morning. About seven. And I went over to Paul…to Mr. Thomas's room, and knocked. And went in. And…"

"And you went in and did some things."

"Yes."

"And your aunt came around and barged in on you two?"

"Yes. That's about it."

"Then what?"

"She was pretty mad. I thought she'd have a heart attack. I was really worried. Mr. Thomas was very calm, though. He sort of took it in stride, didn't raise his voice to her or anything. He got out of bed and used this reasoning tone with her and at the same time was getting his pants on…it was, I can't think of any other way to put it, it was kind of impressive."

Turner had practice getting caught in bed with women. He had his act down pat; he'd be a cinch on the Amateur Hour, if Ted Mack wasn't dead.

"My aunt told me to go home, to go back to bed and… she said…and sleep this time. Real sarcastic. I almost…I hated her when she said that. That's the part that hurts, isn't that silly? That for a second I hated her and I think, I think maybe I even consciously thought it, thought, I wish that fat bitch would go off someplace and die, and… she did."

The girl looked at me blankly, but the blankness quickly dissolved into more tears and I let her cry a while.

"So they were arguing when you left," I said, when it began to let up.

"Yes."

"You know that your friend has flown the coop."

"Yes. I went up to his room. It looked like he left in a hurry."

"It sure did. Then what do you think really happened?"

"I don't know. It was an accident, it had to be. They were arguing and she went storming out of the room and lost her step and...just fell. Maybe? Or...God. Or they came to blows and he accidently slapped her or something and she fell or...I don't know. It's upsetting. It's scary as hell, too."

"Well he's gone."

"Maybe I don't blame him. For going. No. No, that's not right. I do blame him. I wish..."

"What do you wish?"

"I wish I could hate him."

"You want some free advice?"

"I think maybe I could use it."

"Forget about this. It was an accident."

"Do you really think that?"

"I don't know. But I just talked to Charley, and he's very shaken by it. He said he wished this wasn't an accident, so he could have somebody to blame. If he knew about your Mr. Thomas, I'm afraid he'd go looking for him. And kill him."

"Oh...oh. Oh."

"And you wouldn't want that."

"No."

"So sit there and swing and think and then forget."

"And then what?"

"How do you feel about Charley?"

"I've been living with them...Wilma and Charley...for over a year. Since my folks split up. Charley's been good to me. He's a nice man."

"Then help him put his life back together. Help him run that place across the street. For a year or two, and then go about the business of putting your own life together."

"You're a funny one."

"Oh?"

"I think my aunt was right about you. You come on strong, but you're not so tough, really."

"Anything you say. You going to be okay?"

"I guess."

"Okay, then. I'll see you later."

"Will you? I'm going to see if I can't get Charley to open for business again, in a day or so. Come in and maybe we can find out each other's name."

"Maybe. I probably won't be in for at least a week, though."

"Oh?"

"I've got some business to attend to." Some business named Turner.

11

I'd forgotten the cold, back when I was on the porch talking to Wilma's niece, but as I walked home a chill wind blew in off the still half-frozen lake and reminded me. I'd been living in southern Wisconsin for four or five years now, and was used to winter extending itself well into what should've been spring; still, this was unusual weather: by the time I reached my A-frame I'd seen perhaps a dozen fat flakes of snow fall heavily to the ground, fat wet flakes that hit like bird droppings. Somebody didn't know it was April.

It was cold inside the A-frame as well. I built a fire in the conical metal fireplace that took up the far corner and went over to the couch beneath the overhang of the loft and sat.

The stack of girlie magazines (the ones I'd found in Turner's room) I'd been carrying rolled up and stuck under my arm. I now flopped them onto the coffee table in front of me, and a bare-breasted girl with dark hair and very brief bikini bottoms that didn't completely conceal more dark hair was grinning at me with considerably more than friendship in mind, below the word *Hustler.* This was the cover of the magazine on top of half a dozen others, and I started flipping through them, and they were interesting, in a gynecological way, and in one of them I came across an interview with a director of pornographic films.

His name was Jerry Castile.

I glanced at the cover. It was dated May, of this year. Meaning it was the current issue.

I wondered if the story Turner had told me, about his being here to kill Jerry Castile, had been a spur of the moment thing, fabricated out of Turner's recent memory of having seen this particular article. The page where it began had its upper right corner folded down. Perhaps this was part of Turner's research into the mark…

What the hell. I'd already looked at all the pictures.

I leaned back and read.

12

Associate Editor Rick Marshall conducted the following mini-interview with porno director JERRY CASTILE during a lull in the shooting of Castile's current flick, BLUE MOON.

MARSHALL: Jerry, I think our readers would agree that you're one of the biggest names in porno today. Like Damian, the Mitchell Brothers and a few others, your films have had not only box office impact but critical acclaim that has helped hardcore skin flicks reach beyond the raincoat-in-the-lap audience, to a younger crowd, including many couples. Now we hear a rumor that you're planning to leave the field, to direct films for a major studio. Has all the critical acclaim gone to your head? Or have you simply "said it all," as far as hardcore sex flicks are concerned?

CASTILE: Maybe I had an offer I couldn't refuse. Seriously, several major studios have made me offers, and in August I'll be doing a film for American International.

MARSHALL: Then better money lured you away?

CASTILE: Partially. And I'll have bigger budgets, and can make better, and more varied kinds of movies.

MARSHALL: Does that mean you're bored or tired of porno movies?

CASTILE: No, but in porno these days, a lot of risks are involved. The Supreme Court ruling, giving locals the power to pass and pursue their own anti-smut laws, has made it rough to stay alive. It costs money to fight those fucking court cases, costs money to stay in business and out of jail. There's a lot of repression in the air, and I for one find it scary as hell.

MARSHALL: So we can safely assume you won't be doing porn for any major studio?

CASTILE: Nothing hardcore, certainly. It'll be R-rated stuff. A hard R, but nothing X, and certainly nothing triple X.

MARSHALL: Does that mean that *Blue Moon* is your hardcore swan song?

CASTILE: No. I have one other commitment to fulfill. I'll be going to the Midwest in April, to do a film called *Snow Ball*. We've already done some location shooting, here in the East. The rest of the film will be shot in a ski lodge, a wild place, octagonal building, great for camera angles.

MARSHALL: I didn't know any major porno was being produced in the Midwest. Aren't there a lot of hassles involved with shooting porn in that part of the country, particularly in Chicago?

CASTILE: Frankly, yes. It's very underground. A lot of minor stuff is done there, loops, that sort of thing. Actually, I wouldn't be shooting a film in the Midwest at all, except that's where the financing is. And, I was offered that great place to shoot it in, that octagonal ski lodge.

MARSHALL: Who do you have lined up for the film?

CASTILE: We were hoping for Harry Reems, but he's not going to be available. We've got Frankie Waddsworth, and also Candy Floss.

MARSHALL: Is she still in as good a form as she was in *Sensuous Esophagus*? That bit with her giving head and singing at the same time was remarkable.

CASTILE: We already filmed a scene with her and Waddsworth in a ski lift where she yodels and gives head.

MARSHALL: Versatile girl. Sounds like *Snow Ball* ought to be a terrific way to bring down the curtain on your hardcore career.

CASTILE: Well, I won't be going out with a whimper.

13

The temperature seemed to be dropping by the second, and the initial layer of heavy, wet snow, which I had assumed would melt quickly away, was starting to freeze, and now more snow, lighter snow, the stuff that drifts are made of, was covering it over.

Under normal conditions it would have taken fifteen minutes to get to the Mountain. I was lucky to make it there in half an hour. Even in perfect weather these narrow, winding roads were unkind; today they were downright sadistic. And, of course, visibility was next to nil, though I did have the roads pretty much to myself, as very few others were moronic enough to go out in this.

I was, however, able to see the gate that closed off the driveway that started up the huge hill, disappearing into the thickness of fir trees that covered the slope, one or two thousand trees assembled on the hillside like little men waiting for something, this storm maybe, or maybe the Second Coming. I slowed and stopped and was able to make out the sign on the gate, reading MOUNTAIN LODGE, and then another sign, reading CLOSED, and a third, NO TRESPASSING. The gate was barnwood, and so was the fence that extended from either side of the gate, extending along the frontage of the Mountain Lodge property, down to where some non-fir trees separated the Lodge land from the beginning of the yard of a two-story, somewhat rundown clapboard farmhouse. Both the barn-wood fencing and the old farmhouse looked rustically attractive in the falling snow, like something Hallmark set up for the front of a card. Only in this case it would have to be April Fool's.

The farmhouse had a driveway, too, but it wasn't blocked off by a locked gate. There wasn't any gate, nor much of anything else, except the obviously deserted farmhouse, its windows X'ed with wood slats, its paint beginning to peel, its yard overgrown to such an extent the several inches of snow couldn't hide the fact.

I pulled into the driveway, which was loose gravel, and drove around behind the house, where the barn was. The barn was red faded to a coppery orange, except for the side facing the highway, and this at one time had been painted into a billboard for some product, but the lettering and the picture below the lettering were obscured by the years, and the snow.

I got out to see if the barn was locked. Snow kept tossing itself in my face, like handfuls of powdered glass, and the wind pushing me around had teeth in it. But I had on a quilted thermal jacket and an arm to put in front of my face and was protected, though it would've taken an Eskimo suit to really do the job. The nine-millimeter, with its silencer, was stuck down in my belt; the thermal jacket was short-waisted and if I wanted to I could slip a hand easily up onto the butt of the gun. I wanted to, and did. There was a possibility I might find Turner's blue-gray Chevy parked inside the barn, and if so, I might be needing the gun. Soon.

The barn was unlocked. I took a look around, and found it warm, comparatively speaking, and obviously still in use: no expensive equipment in view, but plenty of hay. I would've been surprised had the barn not been in use: a farmhouse might logically be deserted, but the adjacent land wouldn't be. Not in this part of the country. This was apparently one of the many small farms that have been swallowed up by larger ones, leaving the farmhouses vacant, although considering the nearness of the Lake Geneva and Twin Lakes vacation centers, the house was probably rented out in summer.

And possibly in winter, but not now. Not in the off season, in the spring, if this was spring: any robins in the neighborhood when the storm hit were frozen dinners by now.

Turner's Chevy wasn't in the barn. And there wasn't any indication any other vehicle had been, either, with the possible exception of a tractor or something. I would still need to check inside the house itself, I supposed, but the likelihood of Turner being in there, without his car in here, was slight.

But he *would* be holed up in one of the farmhouses nearby, that I felt sure of. He wasn't smart enough to scratch the hit, to get the hell out, which he should've realized was necessary last night, the moment I showed up at Wilma's to hold a gun on him and get him talking.

And now that he'd had a fatal confrontation with Wilma, the hit would seem out of the question; but then he should've been gone before the scene with Wilma had a chance to happen, but he hadn't. The fucking jerk.

I knew how he was thinking. His reasoning would be that neither my showing up, nor the unpleasantness with Wilma, had anything directly to do with the hit, so why not go on as planned? All that would be needed was for him to relocate. He had probably already been using a farmhouse around here as a stakeout point; he'd only been using the room at Wilma's to sleep and bang the niece.

So he'd be around.

Me too.

But I did have one nagging thought: suppose Turner was smarter than I gave him credit for. Or somebody in back of Turner was directing his actions and anticipating mine. I'd become convinced that Turner really was in the area to hit Castile, thanks largely to that magazine he'd left behind, with its conveniently dog-eared page cueing me to the Castile interview, which had seemed to confirm the story Turner told me, under the gun.

It had been that article that led me here: the octagonal ski lodge mentioned in the interview as the location of Castile's new film was obviously Mountain Lodge, a resort that had gone bankrupt before it opened, just a year or so ago. There had been a lot in the press about the place, and anyone living in the area would have to know about it. Of course Turner *had* given me one misleading piece of information—saying the lodge was "back deep in a wooded place," which wasn't entirely accurate—but otherwise I had to ask: had I found my way here, or been led? What if this entire series of events had been planned, and set in motion? What if I were still Turner's target, as I'd originally thought, and this was some screwball, elaborate way of getting me in the sights of somebody's sniperscope?

At any rate, here I was: ready to scale the Mountain and make contact with Jerry Castile.

14

The driveway, after making its forty-five degree angle up the tree-studded incline, opened out onto a wide, flat area at the top of the hill, so that when I emerged I was over on the right-hand side of the plateau. So was the lodge, rising in front of me, out of the blinding snow, like a mysterious modernistic silo.

The closer I got, however, the less mysterious the lodge looked, though it was unusual: the vertical barn-wood siding, which made the four-story building seem taller, gave it a rustic quality; its eight geometric sides gave it a modern look. The result was an ungainly compromise at best: a pioneer's vision of a skyscraper; a barn designed by Frank Lloyd Wright.

It had taken me fifteen minutes to get to this point, fifteen slow, cold minutes, walking into snow that was traveling much faster than I was, as I followed the steep, slick pathway the driveway provided, picking myself up after falling on the cement, and then picking myself up again, and finally deciding to walk on the ground alongside, between driveway and trees, instead.

And now I was at the crest of the hill, and seemed to be in a parking lot, the general shape of which was apparent, despite the snow-obscured landscape, thanks to the two sets of half a dozen streetlights that faced each other on either side of an area in front of the lodge, where three cars, their backs humped with snow, were parked. The lot could've handled perhaps several hundred cars, and these three made a small, strange assembly: an ash-gray Plymouth, a yellow Maverick and a silver-gray Mercedes.

Off to the far right of the parking lot was a small building, sort of a shed with aspirations (it too had vertical barnwood siding). A panel truck was parked alongside the shed. The panel truck was an indecisive blue-green color, with a splotch of red on the side where some lettering had been painted out.

No one in the lodge seemed to have noticed me approaching. Even if they'd been watching for me, I'd have been hard to make out in the heavy, blowing snow. All eight sides of the lodge had, on each floor, large quadruple windows, the center pair apparently sliding glass doors, opening onto shallow, unobtrusive balconies; this gave each room an attractive view, what with trees to the rear and ski slope to the fore, and that much anyway had been intelligent planning on the part of the architect. And right now all of those windows, at least those facing me, which was three and a half walls worth, had curtains closed. There was no reason to think anybody knew I was here.

Which was good, because I had some things to do.

I found the shed unlocked, and inside I found, covered by khaki canvas tarps, a snowmobile and a snow plow, the latter no larger than the former, being basically a little garden tractor with a plow stuck on the front. You've probably seen a snowmobile before, but if not, it's a small open scooter, treads in back, skis in front. Both vehicles had pull starts, plastic handles on ropes, just like a power mower; and with both vehicles the motor could be reached by lifting the seat. I did, and used a small wrench I found in the shed, among various other tools in a trunk-like chest, and removed a pair of sparkplugs from both motors. That made four sparkplugs in all, and these I hid in a jar full of nails sitting high on a shelf in the shed. I put the tarps back over the snowmobile and plow. I hid my nine-millimeter and silencer down deep among the tools in the chest. As I did that, I noticed some wire-cutters and took them out. I looked on the several shelves in the shed and found a healthy roll of electrical tape. I dropped the roll of tape and the wire-cutters into a jacket pocket, where I'd already stowed a screwdriver.

It was warm in the shed, or anyway warmer than outside. Back at the A-frame, when I had dressed for the occasion, it had still been April, remember. The thermal jacket was doing a good job, but I hadn't expected the storm to increase in intensity this way, nor for the temperature to have this nervous breakdown. The cold had been beginning to get to me; my hands were getting numb, and my face was starting to get that weird, hot feeling that precedes frostbite, my earlobes especially. I had some other things to do, out in the cold, so I looked around and came onto a second, smaller chest of tools, garden tools; down among them were some gardening gloves. I put them on.

I left the shed, and headed out into the parking lot. The streetlights were unlit, and the curtains in the lodge windows remained closed, and I felt invisible. I had about fifteen or twenty minutes of work to do; perhaps a little less, if I hurried, and didn't let the snow slow me. One by one I lifted the hoods of the cars. Under each hood I used the screwdriver to undo the clip latches on the distributor cap and pull the rotor off the distributor. It's a small thing, a rotor, a few inches long. But it's a good trick to make a car run without one; and, once removed, it's a good trick to figure out that that's why a car isn't working... that is, if the distributor cap has been put back in place, which of course I did in each instance.

I did the same thing on the panel truck, and slipped back in the shed and hid the rotors in the chest of garden tools.

It took me five minutes to find where the phone line went into the lodge. I went all around the building looking for the thing, and then ended up about where I began, near the parking lot, not far from the shed. Coaxial cable rose from the ground and entered a wall of the lodge, just above the cement of the foundation, into a little junction box. I hoped the ground wasn't frozen, because I needed to yank the cable out a ways. I yanked, and yanked some more, and it finally pulled out a few inches. I cut it way down next to the ground, then put tape over both snipped ends, and taped them back together so that a casual glance, or even a less than casual tug, might not reveal that the black cable had been cut, and shoved the cable back into the ground and shaped snow around it a little, so it wouldn't looked messed with. I probably needn't have bothered: my footsteps had been following me in the snow, but more snow was coming down and the wind blowing it all around anyway, so in fifteen minutes all the tracks would be erased and/or covered.

The wire-cutters and tape and each glove I tossed, one at a time, over toward the shed. The snow would cover them, too.

I was getting cold again.

Time to go in.

15

The snow and wind were ganging up on me behind my back and there was nowhere to hide: I was on a porch of sorts, a landing, but it was very much open-air. I'd found several ways in, but this was obviously the main entrance—big double doors facing the parking lot—and I knocked on one of the twin slabs of thick dark wood and it drank up the sound and I knocked again, harder this time, hard enough for my knuckles to feel it, which considering how numb they were from the cold was pretty hard.

I didn't have long to wait.

My insistent knocking got me an almost immediate answer: the door opened a crack and a sliver of face peeked out at me, in annoyance, or maybe fear. Maybe both. In the sliver of face was an eye, a large round slightly bloodshot eye. Above the eye was a scraggly pale blond eyebrow. Also in the sliver of face was a piece of lip. Above the piece of lip I could see a piece of mustache. Scraggly pale blond mustache.

"We're busy in here," he said.

It sounded silly to me then, and it sounds silly to me now, but that's what he said.

"We're freezing out here," I said.

"We?" he said.

"The editorial 'we,'" I said. "And I can turn that into a pun, if you want to spell it o-u-i."

"What?"

"I'm with *Oui* magazine. They sent me here to do a piece on the film you're shooting."

"What?"

"Some people at Lake Geneva, at the Playboy Club, called the office and said somebody ought to come over and do a piece on the fuck film you're shooting. I'm the somebody they sent."

"It's snowing."

"Out here it's snowing. It's probably nice weather in where you are."

"Smart-ass."

"Look, can I come in? It wasn't snowing when I left Chicago, can I help it I got caught in this shit? Let me in. It's cold."

"Freeze your nuts off, smart-ass. See if I give a shit."

"Are you Castile? You aren't Castile. Get Castile."

He thought about it a while. I could tell he was thinking because the big bloodshot eye blinked a couple times.

"Wait here, smart-ass," he said.

"You talked me into it."

The door closed, and a cold few minutes passed before it opened again. All the way this time.

Castile was standing there, outlined by intense light coming from somewhere deep in the place, standing hands on hips, looking cocky as hell, smiling. I recognized him from a picture that had accompanied the girlie magazine interview. He had puffy, styled red hair and goggle-type glasses with light brown tinted glass. His jeans were fashionably faded, his short-sleeve sweatshirt black with the word DIRECTOR in white letters across the chest. Around his waist was a heavy black belt bulging with square packets; this was a battery belt, giving the wearer a power supply to operate a portable camera. This I found out later, but at the moment it reminded me of the heavy belts they advertise for women to wear around the house to lose weight.

Not that Castile needed to lose any weight: he was a small man, slender, short, but his slightly manic smile spoke of energy. Lots of it. He looked about twenty-five but was older, probably early thirties. He reminded me of Mickey Rooney at the point in his life when he was starting to look wrong for the Andy Hardy role.

I got a good chance to study him like this, because he was waiting for me to say something, and I didn't.

Snow was starting to collect on Castile's DIRECTOR sweatshirt and he seemed to be getting tired of smiling or maybe the cold was getting to him. Maybe he just wanted to get me inside so he could shut the door. At any rate, he finally broke the ice, so to speak.

He said, "What's your name?"

"Jack Murphy," I said.

"Never heard of you."

"If you had, I wouldn't have landed an assignment like this."

"True enough," Castile said, adjusting his smile to one side of his face.

I stood for a while and watched the snow collect on him, like heavy dandruff.

"Well," he said. Irritation starting to show, but the smile constant. "Don't just stand there. Come on in. You're putting me behind schedule enough as it is…though with this shitty snowstorm it doesn't really matter. In, in, in."

I went in.

16

The inside of the lodge was, like the outside, an odd mix of modern and rustic: rough, unpainted barnwood again, with thick shag rust-color carpeting that looked warm and lush and was about as easy to walk across as the Okefenokee Swamp; brown and white furniture set here and there, made out of plastic mostly, transparent tables, a white cylindrical chair with a seat scooped out and filled with a brown-and-white striped cushion, a chair that pleased neither the eye nor, I guessed, the ass; paintings, designy geometric shapes of white and brown and occasionally orange in shiny metal frames, out of place and proud of it, against the barnwood walls.

The entry area had a rather low ceiling, with an open stairway disappearing into it, over on the right, and another on the left, but soon this room opened out into another, larger area, the ceiling suddenly very high: the central section of the building, a good-size room's worth, was a shaft that rose to a skylight, which was stuck up among open beams and currently letting in nothing but darkness, thanks to the snow piled on top.

It was as if the building had been cored like an apple, leaving each of the other three floors exposed and incomplete, a skeletal framework of balcony around each floor, where rooms stood curiously open-faced, fronted by two fairly widespread wooden posts joined by a skeletal railing, though each room had a tan shade, a curtain of canvas or something, that could be pulled down to close off the nonexistent front wall of the room, some of the rooms closed off in that manner now, while others gaped like missing teeth in the grinning skeletal mouths of each floor.

The effect of all this—balconies, stairways, open beams, open rooms—was one of spaciousness but, again, only added to that odd combination of modern and rustic, a projection of coldness, despite the pursuit of warmth.

Speaking of which, warm was definitely not the word for the climate in there, and as I followed Castile toward a brightly lit but still indistinct area ahead, a seeming contradiction to the lodge's otherwise subdued lighting, I said, "Isn't the furnace working, or what?"

Castile grinned over his shoulder at me, briefly, and then let me watch the back of his head as he said, "It gets hot under those lights," and he left it at that.

Soon I saw what he meant.

Down half a flight of stairs, in a sunken living room, before a brown brick fireplace that was roaring and throwing off warmth, a couple reclined on a large light brown imitation animal-fur rug. The guy was big, in several senses of the word: he was about six two, slimly muscular, with longish brown hair and a brown mustache and handsome if unmemorable features, and naked. He was having the act of fellatio performed upon him, or, as we used to say in the service, he was getting blown. The girl doing the blowing was rather large herself: she was perhaps five ten and had a figure that was very slim, very trim, except for breasts so large and firm nature may not have had everything to do with it. Her hair was light blond, and carefully coiffed, and I refer both to the well-sprayed upswept hairdo on her head and her pubic hair, which had been thinned and trimmed and shaped into a heart. She seemed to be pretty, as best I could tell, but then a girl doesn't look her best when she has five of a possible nine inches in her mouth.

The guy was leaning back on his elbows, his head back, the girl in a studied sprawl at his side, leaning over him, and a bald round-faced paunchy man in a gray short-sleeve sweatshirt that said CUBS on it and baggy brown slacks stood operating a massive standing camera over to the left, while a tall, painfully thin young man in a dark blue denim jumpsuit fidgeted behind some lights he would periodically fool with. His hair was pale blond and so was his mustache and he was the guy who'd shown me a sliver of face and not much courtesy at the front door. Over to the far left, sitting at a small table that had been placed in front of a couch that was built into a barnwood wall, a young woman with long dark arcs of hair hiding her face wore headphones and hunched over an oversize tape recorder, from which tangles of wire fell onto the floor and escaped into the maze of various-size wires that coiled around the floor like snakes playing dead.

It was warm here. The warmth came only partially from the fireplace: the rest was the lights. Their warmth was exceeded only by their glare. Glare that was, naturally enough, centered upon the actors on the phony fur rug. The lights, of which there were half a dozen of various sizes, stood on metal folding stands like weird sunflowers, their petals black: round bright circles of light surrounded by flaps of black metal. A microphone hovered above the couple, eavesdropping, as they made their sexual sounds, the guy saying little contented things, making little contented noises, a few of which sounded convincing, but not as convincing as the authentic sucking and slurping sounds the girl provided.

"Cut," Castile said.

The girl wiped off her mouth with the back of a hand, looked up and said, "What about the come shot?"

Castile, either not hearing her or ignoring her, went over to the thin pale blond kid and said, "I'm going to move 'em closer to the fire, over toward the right, and I'm afraid we're going to get some shadow from that boom mike. And I don't want to mess with the lights, so swing the boom out of there and use the shotgun mike on 'em, okay?"

The kid said okay and armed himself with a long narrow metal spear that was, apparently, a shotgun mike.

The girl was standing, now, and had her hands on her hips and didn't seem to remember she was naked. She was, by the way, pretty, now that she didn't have her mouth full.

"Jerry," she said. "I said, what about the come shot?"

"Since when are you looking forward to that?"

"Looking forward to it my butt. I know you, is all. You're going to want a come shot. Right?"

"Right," he admitted. "We'll shoot an insert later on."

"Later on when?"

"Tonight. It's more important we get to the straight fucking, get some good meat shots and save the come shot for the end of the fucking."

"What's the deal?" she said, her mouth on sideways. "Can't this queen get it up again and do 'em both?"

The guy, who'd been leaning back on the rug, to the rear of this discussion, looking bored and a little tired, now sat up and said, "Yeah, and what do you know about it, bitch? All you got to do is spread 'em. *I* do the hard work."

"Well you don't do it hard enough."

"Yeah? Well look what I got to work with."

"You said it, not me."

"You little bitch…"

And the guy was rising. To his feet, that is.

Castile got between them, got caught under the glare of the lights for a moment and pushed his hands out at the air in a conciliatory fashion. "Settle down, kids. Just settle down. Frank, I know you could probably handle doing two come shots in a row, God knows I've seen you do it, but it's just safer, or easier rather, to save the other one for later, as an insert, nice for variety anyway, a nice close-up insert. Now. Can we go on to the fuck scene?"

"Fine," the girl said. "But he can just get himself ready for that insert and bring me in for the finish. We got plenty of blowjob footage as it is already. I'm not doing this for fun, you know. Not with this cheese-brain, I'm not."

"Keep it up, bitch," the guy said, trying to sound threatening and not quite making it.

"Isn't that what *you're* getting paid for?" she said, arching a brow.

"Kids," Castile said. "Please. We've gotten along so well, so far. This is the last day, after all…just this one last tiny fuck scene and one last tiny come shot insert and we're home free. What do you say?"

Silence.

And then, after a good full minute, the girl said, "Okay."

And she smiled at the guy.

He didn't believe her at first, which he shouldn't have, because she was about as sincere as a used-car salesman, only not as good at acting. But then he seemed to buy it. The boy just wasn't particularly bright. He smiled back and said, "All right, baby. Let's show 'em how it's done."

And the girl smiled again, though there was more than a trace of smirk in it, and Castile said, "Roll," to the fat man who stood behind the massive black machine that was bigger than any man in the room, including the guy preparing to ball a very naked and pretty girl, and they were both saying, "One, two, one two," like an after-dinner speaker testing his microphone, while the thin blond kid lurked off to the side with his shotgun mike, and Castile looked over at the dark-haired girl at the tape recorder, who nodded at him, and he stepped momentarily in front of the camera and slapped together a pair of hinged boards, a skinny one on top of the wide one that had data written in chalk on it, and Castile said, "Action," and the couple started fucking.

They started out missionary position and were apparently really getting into it. Both of them were moving together in what seemed to be passion, accompanied by all the appropriate moaning and groaning, and it was amazing how much they really seemed to mean it, especially, surprisingly enough, the girl, who had a very believable orgasm after about five minutes, a screaming, body-shaking orgasm that prompted Castile to come in for some close-up work.

He'd been on the sidelines, waiting to use a small handheld camera with a large magazine that said ARRIFLEX on it, staying out of range of the other, much larger camera, watching the couple on the rug hump each other as if they meant it. He had been, you should excuse the expression, waiting for an opening.

And now he'd found it. He went in for his close-up work, roving around the couple, at one point slapping the guy's naked ass, which had prompted the guy to put his hands under the girl and lift himself and her off the ground, and Castile got down in for some very close-up shots of grinding genitals. When he finished that, he slapped the guy's ass again, and the guy withdrew and turned the girl over, roughly, and entered from the rear. Castile got back out of camera range, while the fire flickered on the sweating naked bodies, and it was real and unreal all at once.

Finally the guy withdrew and laid that slab of nine inch meat across the upper portion of her ass and he came. A long shooting stream of it, and it caught in the girl's hair, and glistened there, surrealistically.

I looked over at Castile and he was grinning. His eyes were glistening in much the same way as the trail of white fluid that had landed and now hung in her hair, like an obscene Christmas ornament.

"Cut," Castile said, softly, with not a little satisfaction.

And, with the camera no longer rolling, the girl began to scream.

"You son of a bitch!" she was saying, in the shrill voice of somebody whose finger got slammed in the door. "You son of a bitch!"

And she threw a nice hard right into the side of the guy's head—he was still on his knees, in dog position—and he went down for the count.

She stood over him, raving and ranting, her hands balled into fists, her naked breasts jiggling, all of her trembling with rage.

"You shit! You putz! You did it on purpose!" She kicked him in the side of one thigh.

"No, no," he said, feebly, afraid the next blow would be more appropriately placed.

"You didn't have to get it in my hair. Do you have any idea how long it takes me to do this hair? And if we're shooting an insert tonight, I'll have to get it ready again, before then, wash it, dry it, set it…ooooh! Get out of my sight, you miserable wimp, before I kick your paycheck up around your ears!"

And the guy got to his feet and, doubled over, did as she told him, pausing only to grab a robe from a chair.

The fat cameraman was laughing. The pale blond kid wasn't. The dark-haired girl was in the shadows.

Castile put an arm around the girl's shoulder. Smiling, he said, "You were a little rough on that poor kid."

"Poor kid my butt. He ever comes in my hair again, I'll kill him."

"Easy, baby. Easy. I want you to meet somebody."

And she noticed me for the first time. She smiled a little, looking me over, and said, "I'm sorry about the way I look," gesturing to her hair.

"Rest of you looks just fine," I said.

"Yeah, well," she said.

"This is Jack Murphy, baby. He's doing a piece on the film for *Oui.* Braved the storm and everything. Jack…is it okay if I call you Jack?"

"Sure," I said.

"Jack," he said, squeezing his star's shoulder affectionately, "I'd like you to meet my wife."

17

The bar was the only room I'd seen so far that revealed the original intention of the place: that is, to be a hotel of sorts, a resort. That's what Mountain Lodge would have been had it not gone prematurely broke. This building was, as I understood it, a prototype, the intention being to put up another one like it on the left-hand side of the plateau, and eventually one or more such buildings at the bottom of the ski slope, over to the sides, one would assume. But the project had never gotten that far: this one building was it, and rumor was that a Chicago businessman bought the place and now used it as a vacation hideaway. Rumor also was the business he was in was the mob.

At any rate, the bar was in keeping with what Mountain Lodge would've been, had it ever opened. It was also in keeping with the lodge's schizoid marriage of rustic and modern: barnwood booths with brown padded seats and backs grew out of barnwood walls, each booth having a clear plastic tabletop on barnwood legs; a large barnwood horseshoe bowed out from the back barnwood wall, which was largely taken up with shelves lined with bottles and glasses; and in the foreground of the room were high round tables with transparent tops surrounded by stools with brown padded seats, similar stools lining the horse-shoe bar.

Castile sat me in one of the booths—the bar was adjacent to the living room where the filming had been taking place—and excused himself; his wife had already said glad-to-meet-you and scurried upstairs to wash her hair.

But the fat guy in the CUBS sweatshirt cornered Castile, before the director could leave the bar area. The thin blond kid made an inadequate shadow behind the fat cameramen, who was asking Castile if he realized just how bad this snowstorm really was.

"I hadn't really thought about it," Castile allowed. "I mean, we been in here filming all day, Harry. Isn't that enough to think about?"

"Well, we're snowbound," Harry said, "and we're not filming now. So maybe you better think about that."

"What can I do about it?"

"You can answer a question. You can tell us whether we get paid for any days we're stuck here in the snow."

"I don't know, Harry. I'm not producing the picture."

"What's that supposed to mean?"

"It means I'm a hired hand just like you. I'm being paid through today...which is our last day of shooting...just like you. It's my tough luck...and yours...if we get snow-bound."

"If, shit. We *are* snowbound. And don't give me that bullshit about you being a hired hand. You got a percentage."

"Sure I got a percentage. But I won't see any of that

money…if there is any…until the film goes into distribution, which is months away. So give me a break."

"Shit."

"Look Harry. I'll talk to the money people and see if we can't get some extra bread to cover any extra time we spend here. But Jesus. It's April. We're not going to be snowbound for long. Overnight, maybe. So what say we all just relax, just, you know, just take it easy."

Harry thought about it, shrugged. A beat later, so did the blond kid, who'd been silent throughout, eyes bouncing from Castile to Harry, Harry to Castile, watching the conversation like a spectator at a tennis match.

Then Castile patted Harry on the shoulder, smiled at the kid, and left.

Harry came over to my booth and looked down at me. He wasn't tall, but he was standing and I was sitting and he took advantage of that. He poked at the table with his belly, accusingly.

"You one of the money guys?" he asked.

"What?"

"You one of the guys putting up the money for this piece of crap?"

"No."

"Then what *are* you doing here?"

"I'm a writer."

"What kind of a writer?"

"I'm doing a story on the film. For *Oui* magazine."

"Oh. Don't use my name in the fucking thing."

"I don't know your name."

"Good. Keep it that way."

"Any special reason you want to stay anonymous, Harry?"

"I thought you said you didn't know my name."

"I don't know anything except Harry, Harry. Sit down. You're making me nervous."

Harry thought about it.

"Hey kid," he shouted, as though the kid were across the room and not just a few feet away. "Go get us some beers, huh?"

The kid went.

Harry sat across from me in the booth.

"Sorry if I came on strong," he said. "I'm a little pissed."

"About getting snowbound and stuck for no extra money."

"That's right. It sucks."

That seemed to me an especially appropriate choice of words, but I didn't say so. I said, "Don't worry. I won't mention you."

"Yeah, well thanks. See, I don't want my name in any article because I'm union and this is a non-union picture."

"Do the unions care if you work on a film like this?"

"Well. Not really. They aren't strict on it. But they say not to use your real name on the production. And it would also hurt the work I do, the other work I do, I mean."

"Which is what?"

"I work with an agency in Chicago. I do commercials, industrial films, straight stuff for straight people. If the people I work for found out I moonlighted doing occasional stuff like this, I'd get my ass in a sling."

The blond kid brought two beers.

"It's the same with Richie here," Harry said. "He works for the same agency I work for. He's a gaffer."

"Gaffer?"

"You know, electrician, does the lights and stuff. Sit down, Richie."

Richie sat down, on the same side of the booth as Harry, who said, "You wouldn't want your name used in no article, would you, Richie?"

"I don't know. I wouldn't mind."

"You'd catch hell if they found out at the agency."

"Fuck the agency." Richie's voice was too young and high-pitched for his words to convey any force. "I'd rather do real films, anyway."

"Shit. You call this crap real films?"

"Jerry Castile is a real director."

I decided to get back in the conversation. I said, "I understand this is Castile's last hardcore picture."

"That's right," Richie said "He's going to be doing some very big things."

Harry shrugged, said, "That's what he's doing now, is filming big things," and he swallowed some beer.

Castile came back, looking irritated.

"The phone's out," he said. "Goddamn storm's worse than I thought."

He sat in the booth, on my side. Just us four boys, in one cozy booth.

"I'll be honest with you, Jack," he said. "I was trying to call the *Oui* offices, to check you out."

I'd guessed as much.

"Oh yeah?" I said.

"Since I can't get through, I'll just have to assume you're for real. But if you aren't…if you're with the police, and God knows we're breaking various nonsensical bluenose local laws in shooting our film…you had best show me your warrant now, and be forewarned that anything you have done or do from here on out is going to constitute entrapment."

"Mr. Castile, I…"

"Jerry. Please."

"Jerry. I'm just a writer. Not a cop. Not even close."

"Good. I'm just trying to be as up front with you as I possibly can. Now. Do you have a tape recorder with you or what? You don't have a pad, I see."

"I'm not going to do any formal interviewing."

"Oh, what is it, then? A reaction piece? Your personal reactions to seeing what goes on on the set of a porno flick, that sort of thing?"

"Right. Behind-the-scenes look and all that."

"You didn't bring a camera?"

"I'm no photographer. Just a writer. I was hoping you'd be able to provide some stills."

"I can do that."

"Fine. You see, Mr. Castile…Jerry…this was very last-minute. I got the call late this morning and just started out driving. By the time I got here the snow was getting out of hand, and I guess I'm stuck here like the rest of you."

Harry belched irritably. The blond kid, Richie, looked

at Harry in a weird combination of admiration and embarrassment.

Castile didn't mind or anyway didn't acknowledge Harry's editorial comment. Instead he looked at me and said, "I don't mean to hassle you, Jack, but I do need to be sure of you."

"I can understand that. I know about the pressures on people in your business these days."

"The fuck film business, you mean. Yes. Which is part of why I'm getting out. Going aboveground."

"Why is that?"

"Hey, fuck films are a dead-end street. Artistically, commercially, every way. And it looks like we're heading into a repressive period again, and people involved in making films like this are maybe going to be tossed in jail. So I've taken an offer from a major studio, and I'll soon be into safer, more rewarding work. More rewarding in every sense of the word."

As he was saying this, the dark-haired young woman who had been hunched over the tape recorder in the adjacent room approached the booth and I got my first good look at her.

She was wearing a dark blue long-sleeve sweater that was somewhat loose but clung nicely to her breasts, which were not large, but were there, bobbling provocatively; jeans clung nicely to the rest of her trim but shapely figure. She wore wire-frame glasses with huge round lenses that dwarfed her small, delicately featured face, giving her a little girl look. Her eyes were large and brown as her hair.

She wasn't as sexy as Castile's wife, but she'd do.

"I couldn't help but overhear," she said, "that we're going to be stuck here overnight."

"Afraid so," Castile said. "Would you call me a chauvinist if I asked you to check out the food situation?"

The girl said, "Yes, but I'll do it," and smiled, and looked at me for the first time, and her smile fell.

She'd just realized something that I had realized a few seconds before, when I got that first good look at her.

We knew each other.

18

Her name was Janet Katz. Her father was Robert Katz, a dentist from Chicago, actually Elmhurst, and he kept a cottage at Twin Lakes, not far from my A-frame at Paradise Lake. Bob Katz was in his mid-fifties and, during the summer, was one of the group of men I occasionally played poker with. As far as he knew, I was a salesman, and on the road a lot. He knew me by the name I used at Paradise Lake, and so did his daughter. And she knew me another way, too.

We spent a night together, at my A-frame, a few years ago. She'd just graduated from the University of Iowa—her father's alma mater—with a degree in TV and Film, and a naive assumption she was going to make it big. She was going to direct movies, she said. She was just visiting her folks, at their lake place, on her way to move in with a friend (whose sex she never specified) in Chicago, where she'd landed a job as a receptionist at a TV station, her hope being to eventually get into the production area. And after a while she'd go out to California and make it big.

But she hadn't gone to California yet, apparently. If she had, she certainly hadn't made it big. Otherwise she wouldn't be here, doing the sound for a porno film.

"This is Janet Stein," Castile said. "Janet, this is Jack Murphy. He's doing a story on the picture, for *Oui* magazine."

We exchanged brief, glazed glances. I made a shrug with my eyes and she tightened her mouth into a sort of smile and it was an agreement not to mention, in front of these people, that the both of us were using phony names.

"Nice to meet you, Janet," I said.

"Same here," she said, weakly.

Weakly, that is, considering Janet Katz, no matter what name she was using, had a rich, baritone voice that wouldn't sound weak on her deathbed. It was one of those almost masculine voices that, paradoxically, can make a woman seem all the more feminine. Another woman I knew, named Lu, had a voice like that, and in the case of both women, I liked the effect.

"I hope you won't consider this a reflection on you, Janet," I said, smiling, "but I suddenly realize I need to be led to a bathroom. How about directing me?"

Janet smiled back, said she'd be glad to, and Castile, before getting out of the booth to let me by, suggested Janet show me to one of the rooms upstairs.

"You're as snowbound as the rest of us," he told me, "so you might as well go ahead and check into this hotel. Each of the rooms has its own private bath."

I thanked him, and went with Janet, who led me across the central open area of the lodge, the snow-clogged skylight above us, to one of the stairways, where I followed her up to the second floor, into one of the rooms, its tan canvas shade already drawn.

The room was what I expected: the side barnwood walls were decorated with abstract paintings in brown and white in metallic frames; the facing wall consisted of quadruple windows, with the center ones sliding glass doors leading out to a shallow balcony, a pattern common to all the rooms, I'd noted from the outside, with a few exceptions (the sunken living room and the bar and a few other first-floor rooms). The windows were frosted over and it was cold in the room, thanks partially to all this glass, but then it was cold everywhere in the building, except under and around the glaring lights required by the filming, and once the filming was done and the lights shut down, I assumed the heat in the place would finally be turned on. In the center of the room was a rust-color couch that would, I suspected, convert to a double bed, like the one in my loft at home. The wall to the right included a door that stood open to reveal the first non-barnwood room I'd seen in the lodge: a sparkling white bathroom. On the right of the door to the bathroom was another door, a closet probably, and on the left was a built-in dresser, pine drawers built right into the barnwood. The ceiling was rather high, open-beamed, and made the room seem larger than it really was.

She stood near the couch, leaning against it, fiddling with one of the arcs of brown hair that framed her pretty face.

"How will this do?" she said, ambiguously.

"Fine."

"My room's next door."

"That's fine, too."

"Do you really have to…" And she gestured toward the john.

"Not anymore. Seeing you turn up scared it out of me."

She smiled a little. First real smile I'd seen from her today. "I'll show you my room."

She did. It was the same as mine, except the couch had already been converted to a bed. A sloppy, unmade bed, at the moment.

"I'm always something of a slob," she said, "when I don't have a roommate."

She sat on the bed. So did I.

"Maybe I can do something about that," I said.

She touched my face. Kissed me. Put her tongue in my mouth.

"You could sleep in here," she said, after coming up for air, "if you'd like."

"I'd like."

"We've got some catching up to do. How long has it been? Two years?"

"About."

"You know, I've thought about you, Jack. Often."

Jack really was the first name she knew me by: it was the Murphy part of the name I was using here that made it phony to her.

"I think about you, too," I said.

And I had, every time I played poker with her father, who had entrusted his daughter to me one evening, figuring I was a safe bet. I was, but he was betting the wrong way.

"I probably shouldn't believe you," she said, stroking my face, "but I think I will."

"Well, why not? We did spend a…memorable evening together, after all."

"Yes. Memorable. Yes. Mmmm."

I'd just slid a hand under her sweater, touching a breast tentatively, its tip poking back at me, but I decided not to take the credit for that: the room was pretty cold.

But I was warming up, so I played with her breasts for a while and she talked.

"Are you really a writer, now? Is 'Murphy' a pseudonym? You can guess why I'm not using my real name. The experience is what I'm after, here, the chance to work with a director like Jerry Castile. He's very good, you know, and getting well known, despite the subject matter of his work. Do that some more. Please. Anyway, this opportunity was just too good to pass up. Look. Let me take my glasses off. Yeah. There. Just put 'em over there, would you? Yeah. Thanks. Mmmm. Listen…my father didn't find out about this, did he? He didn't send you…"

I cupped her chin in one hand. "That's not nice."

"…what?"

"It's not nice to put your tongue in my mouth and tell me how you think about me and let me play with you while you ask if your father sent me to spy on you."

"I just thought…"

"Don't think. Don't bother. I wasn't sent by your father to spy on you. I'm not about to tell him or anybody I saw you here."

"Jack, I didn't mean..."

"Sure you did. But never mind. You owe me nothing, except the courtesy of keeping my real name to yourself. I have my reasons for not wanting it spread around."

"I understand," she said.

"Good," I said.

Of course she didn't understand at all, but that probably hadn't really occurred to her: she was just saying something to say something. And I hadn't had time to make up an effective lie to cover my presence here, so I let it pass.

"Now," I said. "You want your glasses back?"

"Not particularly."

"Fine," I said, and put my tongue in her mouth.

19

"Sorry I took so long," I said, returning to my place across from Castile in the booth in the bar. "I got talking to Janet. Interesting girl."

"Well," Castile said, with his practiced smile, "you must have the journalist's knack for getting people to talk."

"Oh?"

"Janet's been very quiet, on and off the set. Also very efficient, very intelligent…but despite her efforts to seem unimpressed by all the naked flesh and sex-on-camera, I don't believe she's ever worked on anything like this before."

"She admitted as much, when we talked," I said.

"She certainly opened up to you in a way she hasn't for any of us," he said, and that was probably true. "Ah. Here she is now."

Janet came over; looking cool and pretty, and stood with her hands clasped in front of her, fig-leaf style, and gave her report on the food situation.

"There are still plenty of cold cuts left," she said. "And bread. And beer. But that's it. There's a pantry but it's bare."

"We've been having our lunches here," Castile explained to me, "and then having a late supper at a place up the road a ways. Great food. Wilma's Welcome Inn, it's called. That chili there is something else."

"Well," the girl said, "it'll be cold cuts tonight. And beer."

"And bread," Castile said, good-humoredly.

"Mind if I join you?"

The voice came from behind me, but I soon saw who it belonged to: Castile's sex-star wife, who was wearing a green terry-cloth full-length robe, belted at the waist, with a white towel turbaned around her head. She wore no makeup at all, now, and the effect was startling: she was pretty, with a fresh quality, almost an innocence, that seemed incongruous with the image of her I had in mind, which was of her being humped from behind while cameras dispassionately rolled on.

"Sit down, baby," Castile said.

Janet stood aside, so Castile's wife could push through and sit next to him in the booth. Then Janet said she'd go off to the kitchen and make a platter of sandwiches for everybody, if Castile wanted her to, and he did, and she went.

"Doesn't she mind playing cook?" I asked.

"When you're shooting a picture with a crew this small," he said, "everybody has to be ready to do just about anything. Fixing lunch is just one of the jobs that's fallen to Janet. She's been making the sandwiches every day we've been here and hasn't complained yet. And that's three days now."

"Brownie points," his wife said.

"Pardon me?" I asked.

"She's just trying to rack up some brownie points with Jerry. She's as bad as that little nerd over there, what's-his-name, that Richie. Both of 'em got visions of Hollywood in their empty little heads."

"Baby, you're being a little harsh..."

"Not at all. Realistic is all. I bet the little bitch'd take her clothes off in front of the camera if you asked her to." She caught a glint of skepticism in my eye, and said, "You don't think so, mister, uh, what was it?"

"Murphy. And not mister...Jack. And no, I don't think she'd take her clothes off on camera. Not and do the kind of things that'd be expected of her, anyway."

"And why not?"

"She doesn't seem the type."

"Who is? I'd still be running a beauty shop if I hadn't done it."

"Why did you? Money?"

"No, not money. The beauty shop was making money. I guess I got a little exhibitionist in me. I'm no whore, I'll tell you that. I'm an actress. And there is a difference. Sure, I know what you're thinking. I was screwing that guy, and was getting paid to do it. Now a whore will sometimes be something of an actress, I'll admit, and can fool a guy into thinking he's brought her off, that she's really digging what he's doing to her, what she's doing to him. But how many of 'em could hump a turkey like that Frankie Waddsworthless on camera, on cue, on screen, and make it look like she's enjoying it? Having the greatest goddamn climax since the Virgin Mary had the big wet dream?"

Castile seemed a little uncomfortable during this speech. Apparently he didn't want *Oui* magazine to know his wife/star considered the star of the picture a turkey.

"And speaking of Frankie," she said, now talking directly to her husband, "I've decided I don't want to shoot that insert this evening. Maybe tomorrow morning."

"Now, baby…"

"Jerry, please. When I washed my hair, my makeup got messed up, and so I took a shower, and I'd have to start all over again with the makeup, and…" (She spoke to me now.) "…and on a fuck movie makeup is a real nightmare. You got to go the whole glamour route, foundation, eye makeup, nails, and then body makeup, some of it going in places where you don't generally put makeup, I mean, when you get your tits, among other things, blown up the size of a steamship on some movie screen, makeup is pretty important, believe me, and…" (She spoke to Castile.) "…I just can't bear to go through that whole trip again. Not when I know what's waiting for me when I get there. Please. Maybe tomorrow morning. What the hell, we're snowbound anyway."

Castile thought about it. His ever-present smile was not present, however, when he nodded assent.

"Thanks, doll," she said and gave him a peck on the cheek.

"I'll go tell him," Castile said, gesturing for her to get out to let him out, which she did, and he put his smile back on long enough to shrug goodbye to me, and left.

His wife got back in the booth.

"My movie name is Helen Ready. That's R-e-a-d-y. My real name is Mildred Castile. Glad to meet you."

She extended a small, almost dainty hand and I shook it.

"My husband's a little upset with me, I think," she said.

"Because you don't want to shoot that scene."

"That, and because I got a big mouth. I mean, he'd rather I put on a front for you, since you're a media person and all."

"Your front looks okay to me."

"The back ain't bad, either, but that's something else I don't do that my husband would probably go for."

"Pardon?"

"He'd probably like me to come on to you and take you off in the bushes somewhere and give you something to remember me by."

"I was just making a smart remark. I wasn't coming on to you, Mrs. Castile."

"Millie, please. No, I know you weren't, but I was just trying to get back on a subject we were talking about earlier, which is my being an actress and not a whore. See, my husband thinks that since there's nothing wrong with me humping on screen, why not hump an occasional media guy for a little better press, you know? Only familiarity breeds contempt and I don't think giving the boys in the press room a free ride would do my career any good, and certainly not my husband's. I mean, I would think it would tend more to make media people contemptuous of him, and do his career harm in the long run."

"You're certainly frank about all this."

"Which is what makes my husband upset with me. He's afraid you'll put every word I say into your article. Will you?"

"I don't know. Maybe. Do you want me to?"

"I don't know. Maybe." She smiled. Very genuinely, showing her gums. "All this frank talk may be a front after all, huh? Just my way of catching your imagination and getting some play in your magazine? And without even once going into the bushes with you."

We both laughed a little at that, and I said, "You said before you ran a beauty shop. Do you mean you worked in one, or managed it, or what?"

"I owned it. It was my family's. My folks and my only sister got killed in a plane crash when I was in high school. So I inherited the family business. An aunt helped me run it. She ran it solo, while I went to beauty school. Why? That's certainly boring stuff. Does *Oui* want that?"

"I don't know. I'm just interested. What about your husband? How did you meet him?"

"Well, he's older than me, I'm just over thirty. He's in his thirties, too, but closer to forty. He was managing a restaurant in the same neighborhood…this was in New York…and we were going together. He was into old movies, was taking some courses at a college, not going for a degree or anything, just taking courses, anything to do with film. I was bored with what I was doing. I'd done some little theater-type stuff, and high-school drama before that, and liked it, liked it a whole lot better than doing somebody's hair. Always did have stars in my eyes, I guess, and so Jerry and me hit it off, and he'd heard about the porno stuff people were doing, a lot of it was on the West Coast, nothing too good was being done in the east, so we decided to get into it. I financed it…I had money, from my parents, and I have an uncle who's a soft touch, and is to this day…and we started making movies, That's, what…maybe five years ago. And we both always figured we'd use it as a springboard…never had any intention of staying in porno. We always knew we'd go aboveground. And it's finally happening."

"You mean the contract your husband signed to do a movie for American International."

"Well, it's really more than that. It's got options that make it a multi-picture contract, really. It's the big time, it really is."

"What about you? Your movie career?"

"I'll be in everything Jerry does. You just saw me shoot my last fuck scene, kiddo. I may take my clothes off on camera again, but it won't be to do anything obscene."

There was a sort of logic to that that was somehow irrefutable.

Across the way, in another booth, Richie and the fat cameraman, Harry, were sitting, talking. Or anyway Richie was talking. Harry just sat and scowled. Richie seemed a little frayed around the edges; he was waving his hands a lot and maybe was thinking about crying. I couldn't hear anything they were saying: the one-sided conversation was intense but the volume was low.

"Lover's quarrel," she said, noticing me watching the two men.

"That so?"

"Yeah. I think Richie was in the sack with Frankie last night, and Harry found out, and brother."

"Oh. Is everybody around here queer?"

"Not me. But I'm a married lady. If you're horny, you'll have to take a shot at Janet." And she smiled. "That's a laugh. If you can get that cold little bitch in the sack, you can have me for dessert, married lady or not."

I was tempted to take her up on that. She was, after all, one of the best-looking women I'd ever seen. And I liked her. For an actress, she was remarkably honest.

But that had been her exit line; she rose and swayed off, and just as she did, fat Harry rose and left his friend Richie alone in the booth.

So I joined him.

20

“Mind if I join you?” I said.

The kid looked up, smoothed the front of his demim jumpsuit absent-mindedly. He pursed his lips, which made his scraggly blond mustache quiver like a caterpillar thinking about starting its cocoon. Then he looked down again, and muttered, “Go ahead.”

He sat with his elbows on the booth’s transparent plastic tabletop, heels of his hands pressed to his forehead.

I sat across from him and waited him out. I think he wanted me to start, wanted somebody to ask him what was wrong, to make sympathetic sounds. I’m not particularly good at sympathy, so I waited him out.

“Ever had one of those days?” he finally asked, peeking out at me with those slightly bloodshot eyes, between the heels of his hands.

“Get out of the wrong side of the bed?” I asked. Innocently.

“You can say that again.”

I decided not to.

“I’m a screw-up,” he said, lowering his hands. “It’s that simple.”

I couldn’t see arguing with him. He’d been a real asshole

when he'd met me at the door; I was still holding that against him.

Which happened to be the subject he started in on, to illustrate that he was a screw-up.

"Like when you came to the door," he said. "I misjudged you. I thought you looked...I'm sorry...but I thought you looked suspicious. I know that's silly. You're a very normal-looking guy. I mean, nice-looking, even. But I misjudged you. Screwed up."

"It's okay," I said. Not meaning it.

"No, really. I mean, if I'd known you were from *Oui* magazine..."

"You might not've called me 'smart-ass' so many times?"

"I had that coming. Go ahead. Lay me out."

"No thanks."

"Look, I...I'm glad you sat down. I'd like to start over."

"I only sat down because for my article's sake I need to get to know everybody involved with the filming...including you. But according to what your friend Harry said, I guess you might not be too willing to talk to me. He doesn't seem to be."

"Harry just doesn't want it getting out he's done a porno. He...he just doesn't understand."

"What doesn't he understand?"

"A lot of things. Jerry Castile, for one. Harry doesn't understand *who* Jerry Castile is. All Harry can see here is a porno film being shot. He doesn't see this for what it is."

"What is it?"

"Film." He said it almost religiously.

"I see."

"Castile is...he's a director. What more can I say?"

"Not much."

"That's right. After you've said it...after you've seen him for what he is...a director...it makes all the difference. Subject matter, what's that? It's not substance that counts. It's style. Look at Howard Hawks."

"What?"

"Look at Howard Hawks. He did westerns, he did comedies, war pictures, a private eye picture, crime pictures, but in them all, through them all, he was Howard Hawks."

"I can't argue with that," I admitted.

"Look at Hitchcock," he went on. "Suspense films. That's what the public thinks of when they think of Hitchcock. But is it the subject matter of those films that's important? No. It's the style. It's Hitchcock."

"That's a real good point."

"I could make the same point about Alan Dwan, Fritz Lang, Samuel Fuller, a dozen others."

"I'm sure you could."

"They'll be doing books on Castile someday. This period...the sex films...will be just one small, if interesting, part of his *oeuvre*. He'll go on to do other films, initially simple genre pieces, I'm sure, but whatever he does, he'll remain one thing, essentially...Castile."

"And a director."

"Yes! A director. Might I say...an *auteur*?"

"You might."

"I'm glad you understand what I'm getting at. It's so frustrating to talk to someone like...like Harry, who just can't see the forest for the trees."

"It's hard, in a snowstorm."

"Yes," he said, smiling solemnly, nodding, finding several layers of meaning below the surface of my flip remark. If I'd said it before, when I was some guy knocking at the door, he'd have called me "smart-ass" and let it go at that; now that I was with *Oui*, I was suddenly deep.

He leaned in close to me, across the plastic tabletop; he was wearing cologne that smelled like fruit, and I resisted the temptation to look for any layers of meaning in that. "Harry doesn't understand," he said, "what a rare privilege it is to work with a director of Castile's standing. And this particular film is particularly important."

"Why's that?"

"It's Castile's last sex film, and as such is, well, historic."

"Then I take it you don't have the reluctance to have your name seen in print, regarding this film, that your friend Harry has."

"Not at all. The name is Richard Hudson. H-u-d-s-o-n."

"Is that your real name?"

"Legal name. I had it changed."

"From what?"

"From," he said, coyly, "something I didn't like."

I let that pass, asked, "If Castile is such a meticulous filmmaker, why is he working with such a small crew?"

"Well, we did have some other actors here, but they finished their scenes and left yesterday. And actors, on a film like this, assuming they aren't superstars like a Frankie Waddsworth, will often help with the technical side of things, when they aren't in a scene. But this is a small crew...normally, a picture like this would probably require, oh, twice as many people...but the difficulties of lining up good people, in Chicago, willing to work on a film like this, well...it limited Mr. Castile. But then he has a reputation for working with a smaller crew than most. Does a lot of his own camerawork...all the handheld stuff. That's how he helps retain control, puts his personal stamp on every frame of film. He even does his own cutting and editing as well. Part of his reputation comes from the quality he has been able to achieve on very low-budget productions. He's doing quality comparable to Radley Metzger...the hardcore films Metzger has done he's done as 'Henry Paris'...and Castile's budgets are far smaller, perhaps a third as big."

"And that's one reason the Hollywood people want him."

"Yes. You, obviously, can see what this could mean, working with Castile, and at this point in his career...but Harry can't seem to grasp it. He doesn't see how this could open so many doors. If Mr. Castile should happen to like my work, or Harry's for that matter, we could be in California shooting *film* in a matter of months, weeks, days! We could leave commercials, industrial films, pornography, all the demeaning shit behind, and do *real* films."

For a moment I wondered what happened to the triumph of style over subject matter, but never mind.

"Harry's a good friend of yours, I take it. His opinions seem to mean a lot to you."

"I'm not afraid to tell it like it is."

"That's admirable. What is it?"

"I'm...bisexual. A lot of people in the arts are."

"There's a lot of it going around."

"Yes, and there's nothing wrong with it."

"I didn't say there was."

"I don't mean to be...defensive. I didn't imagine you'd be terribly shocked by my admission."

No, nor interested. But I said, "We run pictures of women together, in *Oui.* People are getting more open-minded on the subject," and hoped that would mollify him.

"Harry and I met through our work...we both work for the same agency, doing, as I said, commercials and industrial films and so on. And despite his Archie Bunker-ish exterior, Harry is a sensitive man, intelligent, and a little enigmatic. We've been...together...for six months now. But he's very possessive."

"Is that right?"

"He'd even be upset if he saw us talking. He's that small."

"Size isn't everything."

"Last night, I...well, I got a little something going with Frank. You know...Frankie Waddsworth, the star of the picture."

"Frankie Waddsworth likes boys?"

"*And* girls. *Bi*-sexual. Bisexual. There's nothing wrong with it."

"I still didn't say there was."

"That's good, because there isn't. And there's nothing wrong with…having a little interpersonal relationship now and then, is there?"

"Not as far as I'm concerned."

"I mean, I shouldn't be telling you this, but, as I said, I tell it like it is…and if you want to print it in your magazine, so be it. I won't try to stop you."

"Thanks."

"So Frankie and I, we were kind of fooling around, and things got out of hand, and Harry butted in. Made a scene. It was ugly, I don't mind telling you. Can't he understand? Frankie Waddsworth isn't just anybody. He's a superstar."

"Superstar?"

"He's been in movies with every major porno actress. And after all of that, he still had time for me. Can you imagine how that made me feel?"

"Not exactly."

"And, so, now Harry is angry with me. I wish I could make him understand."

"Has anything like this ever happened before?"

"No. Not with Harry and me. Though he's always been the possessive type. That's hard to cope with, sometimes, and anyway, who can resist a superstar?"

I couldn't argue with that.

Then Janet appeared, with a platter of sandwiches, which she set on the bar, and everyone—except Frankie Waddsworth—appeared to get something to eat. With the arrival of Harry, Richie and I parted company, so as to not further aggravate the situation, although later I saw Richie sneaking off with some extra sandwiches tucked under his arm, probably going up to serve Waddsworth his supper in bed.

Janet and I shared a booth. The sandwiches were good. They were on rye and mine was corned beef and Swiss cheese. There was beer, too. Olympia and Budweiser. I chose Oly, which is Clint Eastwood's favorite. Who can resist a superstar?

Castile was sitting with his wife. His brown-tinted goggle type glasses were gone, now. Apparently that was part of his directing costume that he discarded when shooting for the day suspended. He was still wearing the DIRECTOR sweatshirt, though.

I had to get him alone and talk to him. Soon. Before Turner beat me to him.

21

After everyone had had their fill of the sandwiches and beer, Castile disappeared upstairs with his wife. I was starting to think there was no way to get him by himself, and I couldn't say what I had to say in front of his wife.

There were several small lounge areas on the first floor, most of them living rooms on the order of the sunken one, though without fireplaces, and dominated by the large windows that were standard throughout the lodge. The windows were draped, but looking behind the drapes you could see frost and nothing much else.

Castile or someone had turned on the heat, but it was still a little chilly. I told Janet that everybody seemed to have guessed that she and I had a natural rapport, and so she consented to share a couch with me, and we snuggled together, there, in a cooperative effort to battle the cold and watch some television.

Castile came in, after a while, sat in a soft chair near the couch, asking if we minded the intrusion: the movie we were watching was *His Girl Friday*, one of his all-time favorites. Howard Hawks directed it, he said. I was tempted to go looking for Richie to tell him.

But everyone besides Janet, Castile and me had disappeared to private cubbyholes in the big lodge.

And after we had watched a second movie, a James Cagney gangster opus called *Kiss Tomorrow Goodbye*, which was not directed by Howard Hawks (I asked Castile), Janet said she was getting sleepy and was going to head on up to her room. I gave her a look that told her I'd be up later. She gave me a look that told me she understood my look, and went on up.

"I didn't know you were a movie buff," Castile said.

The room was dark, except for the TV screen, which right now was between movies, and a long commercial about getting your car repainted was playing.

"I'm not," I said. "But I stay up watching them all night sometimes. The box can be hypnotic."

"It can at that."

"I wonder if we could skip the next movie, though. I'd really like to take a few minutes and talk to you."

"More interview material? Can't that wait till tomorrow? We'll probably be snowed in all day, plenty of time for that then. There's another Cagney coming on in a few minutes…"

"This is something else. Something completely different than an article for *Oui* magazine. It's something important."

"Well. Go ahead, then."

"The telephone isn't out because of the storm."

"What? What are you talking about?"

"I cut the wire."

"You cut the wire?"

"I cut the wire."

"What are you..."

"I'm just trying to make a point."

"Which is?"

"How easy it was I got in here. How quick you've been to buy my story."

"You're not a writer."

"No."

"Who are you, then? You're not a cop of any kind."

"No, I'm not. I'm somebody can help you. That's what I'm here for, really. To help you."

"That's funny. You don't look humanitarian."

"I'm not. I'd make a profit on this deal, hopefully."

"This is the most convoluted approach to blackmail I ever heard of..."

"It's not blackmail, and it's not a confidence game or anything like that, either. I'm here to offer you a service."

"And that service is?"

"A kind of bodyguard, I guess. What would you say... and I know this may sound sort of crazy, but bear with me...what would you say if I told you someone was going to kill you? Not *try* to kill you...but kill you. A professional job, bought and paid for. What would you say?"

"Is that what you are? You're here to kill me?"

His reaction threw me a little: he was taking it so cool... apparently he didn't believe me, thought I was a nutcase.

I tried to straighten him out.

I said, "If I were here to kill you, you'd be dead now."

"I see."

"You haven't answered my question."

"Your question…?"

"What would you say if I told you someone was coming here to kill you? Probably tonight?"

And then he surprised me. He said, "I'd say I believe you."

22

"I guess we both have some explaining to do," he said. His smile was natural, for a change; and he looked older, now, less like Andy Hardy and more like the nearly forty his wife said he was.

"Why don't *you* start," I suggested.

"I thought you might say that. Suppose I tell you some of it. And then you can tell me who you really are, and how you've come to be here."

"Fair enough."

He leaned back in the chair, looked toward the television. The second Cagney movie had begun, a western of some sort, from the 1950s, with Cagney looking heavy and somewhat long-in-the-tooth, and the sound was still on, and it made it a little difficult to hear what Castile was saying. But it was worth the effort.

"Six months ago I received a phone call," he said. "Three o'clock in the morning, give or take a few minutes. As it happens I was up, working on one of my films, using a Movieola to check on some editing problems...a Movieola is a...well, never mind what it is. That's not important. What's important is the phone call."

He paused. Swallowed. Went on.

"It was a man's voice, on the other end. Very average sounding. Perhaps a little on the high-pitched order. And there was a tremor in the voice, but it wasn't nervousness…it was something else. Something else.

"He said, 'I'm sorry to wake you.'

"I said, 'You didn't. I was up already. Who is this?'

"He said, 'I'm nobody you know. And we'll never meet.'

"I didn't know what to make of that. I said, 'I'm hanging up…'

"He said, 'Don't. I have something to say that you'll find…noteworthy.'

"I said, 'What is it, then?' Impatient.

"He said, 'I killed you this afternoon.'

"And I said, 'What?' And then I said I was hanging up again.

"'Don't,' he said. 'It's true…I killed you. I arranged to have you killed, I should say. Took a contract out, just like the movies, just like TV. Hitmen. All of that.'

"I was frightened now. There was something in the voice that was…*real.* It wasn't a crank call. It was real. 'Who is this?' I said.

"And he laughed at me. I asked again, 'Who is this?'

"'My name is Meyers. You'll see my name in the papers, tomorrow, perhaps.'

"'I don't know any Meyers,' I said.

"'I'm nobody. But I'm big enough a nobody to get my name in the papers, when I kill myself.'

"I didn't say anything: I felt like somebody had hit me in the stomach. Hard.

"'You heard right,' he said. 'I'm going to kill myself, tonight. In just a little while. I'll still be on the phone with you, when I do it.'

" 'Please,' I said. Not knowing what else to say.

" 'You'll be dead, too, soon. The men I hired will kill you, one of these days. But you won't know when. Tomorrow maybe. A week from tomorrow. A year from Christmas. One of these days. You'll be dead. They'll kill you. And I'll be dead. We'll all be dead.'

" 'Why?' I asked. Out of breath, hardly getting it out. 'Who am I to you? What have I done to you?'

"And he said, 'I'm cutting my wrists now...' and I heard him make little sounds in his throat; sounds of pain but it was weird, because they were sounds of contentment, too, and he said, 'I'm bleeding now. I'll be dead soon. Like you.' "

And Castile sat staring at the television, where Cagney was shouting at a ranch hand, the images on the screen making shadows on Castile's face, putting emotion on a face that was otherwise a mask at the moment, though his eyes flickered, moved, with something. Something.

"What happened then?" I asked.

"Then he hung up."

"I see. *Was* he in the papers, next day?"

"Yes. Boston papers. He was a mob guy. Fairly high-up. In his fifties. Glorified bookkeeper. He'd cut his wrists, all right. Story even said he was found with the phone receiver in his hands...they assumed he'd changed his mind, at the last moment, tried to call for help."

"And he never said why? He never told you why he hired the contract?"

"No. But I found out. I put some people on it. I have a few connections, myself. My father was involved with mob people, peripherally, and I have some friends in those circles. New Jersey and New York people, but they could find things out for me, about Boston. They found out why the contract was taken out. They also found out it would be impossible to stop what Meyers put in motion. Or damn near impossible."

"What was the reason, then?"

"For the contract? I'd prefer not to go into that. Not until I've heard something from you."

It was my turn, and since he'd given me what was apparently the truth, I gave him the truth back…somewhat edited, of course.

"I'm here," I said, "because I followed a man named Turner here. He's the back-up for the person who's going to hit you. Try to hit you, at any rate. With my help, you might be able to avoid that."

Castile thought about that a second.

Then he said, "Where's this Turner now?"

"Holed up in one of the farmhouses near here, I'd guess. The snowstorm caught him as much by surprise as it did us."

"And how'd you happen to be following this Turner?"

"I used to be in the business."

"What business?"

"Turner's."

He thought about that, too, but longer than a second.

Then he said, "I see."

"Yes, I think you do."

"But you aren't in that business any longer."

"Not exactly. Now I'm in the business of offering my services to the prospective victims…the targets of people like Turner."

"So you followed Turner to this…job…and ascertained that I was the victim, the target, and now you're making contact with me, to do what?"

"To save your life. To stop Turner. And his partner. Usually I make an attempt to find out who took the contract out, as well, since the real threat is the person who sent the hitmen, not the hitmen themselves…in most cases, that is. In your case the guy who bought the hitmen is already known to you, and, better yet, is dead. So once the hitmen are taken out, you can rest easy."

"This is pretty bizarre."

"So are phone calls at three in the morning from guys who slit their wrists as they say they're having you killed."

"But you believed that story."

"Yes. And you believe mine."

"Yes. Bizarre as it is, or possibly because it is so bizarre, I believe you. I do have some questions, though…first, what's your fee?"

"Eight thousand dollars."

"How did you arrive at that figure?"

"It's about what I'm guessing Turner and his partner were paid."

He nodded, as if to say, "Fair enough," then said, "Do you have any idea who the partner is?"

"Yes. I think the partner is in this lodge. Right now."

"What, in hiding…?"

"In a manner of speaking. It's one of your crew."

"What? But that's..."

"Possible. Very possible. Not your wife. Probably not Janet, either...though lady hitmen do exist, believe me. But more likely one of the boys...Frankie Waddsworth, Richie Hudson, or Harry..."

"Not Waddsworth. I've worked with him before."

"That would make it less likely. But not impossible. Most people in the murder business have other jobs, for a cover, for extra income, or both. Waddsworth might have been assigned this *because* you've worked with him, and he'd make a good inside man. Did you go after him, for this film, or did he approach you?"

"His agent approached me."

"There...you see. Waddsworth is a possibility."

"I've never worked with the others before...Hudson or Janet Stein or Harry..."

"Did you approach them?"

"I put feelers out to try and find people, in the Chicago area, who could do the quality of work I need, and who were willing to do porno. It was Richie who contacted me, told me about his agency. Janet I just picked up recently, when our original soundman backed out. She was a friend of a friend of somebody at the Geneva Playboy Club."

"The soundman backing out could've been arranged. That makes even Janet a possibility. What about the actors who finished filming and left yesterday? Had you worked with them, before?"

"Yes, and we drove them into Chicago, to O'Hare, last

night…I saw them board a plane, to go back to New York. So it isn't one of them…waiting behind, lurking in the snow or something. Jesus. This is crazy."

"Naturally. Let me ask you a question. Who would logically be the last to leave this place, once filming is done?"

"Why, me, of course. I'm the director. I'm in charge."

"Well, then, that's when it was supposed to happen. Just you alone here, with that last remaining person, who'd then do you in. Or it's possible Turner would be the one to do you in. It's possible, come to think of it, that Turner is the hitter, and the inside man is the back-up person, the stakeout guy. Very possible. Anyway, that's when it would be done: when nobody else was here. Except you. And your wife, who might also get taken out."

"No!"

"That's the facts of life. But this snowstorm…it's gummed up the works for Turner and company. As long as we're snowbound here, nobody's going to die. Not unless Turner and his partner are willing to snuff all of us, and that's not likely…people in this line of work don't kill unnecessarily. Only when they are paid to kill somebody is somebody in danger, and you're the only one in this place that has a contract out on him."

"But you said my wife…"

"Yeah, she'd probably get her lights put out, too, because she'd be in the way. But that would be a necessary killing, and anyway, with a husband and wife, it would be easy to rig something, easy to make it look like they took each other out."

"God! You make it sound so clinical...like a goddamn textbook."

"Maybe I ought to write one. So. Now it's your turn."

"What?"

"About the contract. About why the guy took the contract out on you."

And he told me.

23

"He thought I killed his daughter," he said.

"I see."

"No you don't. He was wrong. You see...it's hard to explain. Have you heard of snuff movies?"

"Sure. That's where somebody is actually killed on camera, right? Snuff flicks. While back, there was a lot in the press about them."

"Right. Snuff movies, slasher movies, they called them. Most of it was media hype, and I'm glad to say it finally died...pardon the expression. The media finally decided the slasher movies were a hoax...which to a large extent they were. There were some fake ones, but there were some real ones, too. Rumor has it the Manson clan made some, but none of the media people ever turned one up. But I did. Not the Manson snuff movies. But there were a few made in Mexico. Rumor said South America, but it was Mexico. There were four or five of 'em, I found. I bought 'em from a guy...I didn't even buy them, exactly. I was just a middleman. Jesus. It's hard to explain."

"You're doing fine."

"Well, like I said before, I know some people in mob circles, some of my backing's been from them. Like for example, the guy that owns this place, this lodge, he's a mob-related guy. He's backing the picture, and one thing he insisted on was we use his place for some of the filming…he's going to get off on having a print of a porno film shot in this lodge, his lodge, and he can show it to his friends and his girlfriends and everybody can get off on it. Anyway, I was doing a favor for some mob people, being a middleman on these slasher flicks. See the goddamn things don't go into any kind of wide distribution or anything. They're too fuckin' hot for that. But these hardcore violence freaks, these S & M guys, they'll pay incredible coin for something like that. One print, going into a private collection and not likely to be seen by anybody but that one collector and maybe some of his pervert friends, is going to bring in maybe ten grand. Ten grand for a little reel of fuckin' film! It boggles the mind. So I was a middleman for the things, and one of them somehow got seen by this guy Meyers. It was the film that was getting the most attention, of the five or six I handled. Going for something like twelve grand a shot. That was because all the other films had Mexican girls in it. This one had an American. You know how those films go, don't you? They're regular porno loops. Except different. The girl thinks she's just there for the regular sex stuff, sucking, fucking, but then after the sex stuff, right at the climax, the guy, and maybe some other guys who come in the room, takes a razor or something and kills the girl. *Really* kills her. On film. It's something. In some of 'em they dismember the girl. It's something."

"Something," I said.

"Well this guy Meyers, he sees the one with the American girl in it, and he's outraged and he uses his own mob connections to track down the source of the film, and I'm the source, and so he puts the contract out on me."

"The girl in the film?" I said.

"Yeah," Castile said, the images from the TV wavering across his face, "you're right. Just my luck. Meyers's daughter."

24

We talked about a number of things after that. One of them was money: I told him how I wanted to be paid—one thousand now, the rest later—and he liked that, liked the idea of not having to pay any more than that up front, since it showed I had faith in my ability to keep my end of the bargain, to keep him alive so that I would eventually get the rest of the money. I explained that while the later payments should be cash, the first thousand needed to be a check (it's necessary for me to report *some* income to the IRS each year) and went into other details about how the check was to be handled, which I won't go into here.

Another thing we discussed was what he'd been doing to protect himself.

"I'm carrying a gun," he explained.

"Where?" I asked. Even in the dim light cast by the TV screen, it was apparent he wasn't concealing a weapon in an outfit that still consisted of a sweatshirt with the word DIRECTOR on it and jeans, same as he'd been wearing when we met hours before.

"It's in my suitcase," he said, sheepishly. "I know what you're thinking…lot of good it's doing me there. I can see it now, me saying, 'Excuse me, while I go get my gun out of my suitcase.'"

"Not at all. You can't go around with a gun on you while you're working on the film set. You wouldn't need it, anyway."

"Are you armed?"

"I left my gun outside."

"Shouldn't you get it?"

"Nothing's going to happen tonight."

"How can you know that?"

"Hey, I been through this with you before, Castile. Pay attention: we're snowbound here, and unless Turner and his partner want to kill everybody in the place, you should be safe. And I can't see Turner or any pro doing that."

"He could sneak in during the night and then leave."

"Then we'd be snowbound with a corpse and we'd all have to stick around while the authorities looked into it."

"Why would that matter to this Turner?"

"Because he'd be leaving his partner behind. As a suspect. I'm not saying we shouldn't take precautions. Turner's an idiot, and he might try to fake your death to look like an accident or something."

"Jesus. What can we do?"

"Wait a minute…"

"What…?"

Footsteps were echoing in the nearby open shaft area, and I put my hand up to silence Castile.

"Jack…?" The voice was Janet's.

She was wearing a robe, a thin flowered robe that obscured her good figure, and she didn't have her glasses on; she looked sleepy, as if she'd just woke up. Or somebody woke her up.

"Can I talk to you a moment, Jack?"

"Sure. Excuse me, Castile."

I took Janet by the arm and walked her into the adjacent room, another living-room area, where we stood in the darkness and spoke.

"I'm afraid," she said.

"What?"

"Afraid. I don't know why, exactly. I just woke up and was afraid."

"What woke you?"

"I thought I heard voices."

"Castile and I were talking."

"I don't think you're what I heard. I know, I know, I'm only one level up from here, and the rooms are sort of open...but I don't think you're who I heard. The sound came from above."

"Are some of the others sleeping on the upper floors?"

"Yes."

"Then that's what it was. Somebody upstairs from you, talking."

"Maybe I dreamed it. It sounded like...arguing."

"Maybe it was. Harry and Richie and Waddsworth have a little triangle going, I understand."

"I've noticed. So it was them, maybe."

"Maybe. Probably."

"Fine, but I'm scared. I woke up alone and was scared, that's all. I expected you to be there. You said you'd be coming up."

"It's only been an hour or so since you went up, kiddo. I'll be up soon."

"Okay. I'm sorry to be a baby." She gave me a kiss. A nice one. Just a little bit of tongue, this time, teasing.

"I'll be up," I said.

She touched me.

"You're up now," she said.

"You're not scared, you're just horny."

"Maybe that's it," she said, and I could sense, if not entirely see in the unlit room, her pretty smile.

"Shoo," I said.

She let go of my hand, slowly, and drifted reluctantly off, disappearing into the dark.

I rejoined Castile.

"What was that all about?" he said.

"She was just wondering when I was going to come up."

"I see. Is there any possibility…"

"That she isn't the sweet child she seems to be? Sure. I told you before: there *are* women in Turner's business."

"You don't think she's been listening or anything…"

"I don't know. I don't think so. But I don't know."

"Are you sleeping with her tonight?"

"I'll be in the same bed. I'm not going to be getting any more sleep tonight than you, though. Where's your room, anyway?"

"Not near Janet's. It's on the third floor."

"I'll move Janet and me next door to you and your wife. How'll that be?"

"That'll be fine with me. Is that one of the precautions you were talking about taking?"

"Yes."

"What will you tell Janet?"

"I don't know yet, something. But we'll be next door. Count on that. How much does your wife know about all this?"

"Well…she knows I was involved with those slasher films, as middleman…and about the three o'clock phone call from the guy saying he…but I never told her about the relationship between the slasher films and that guy, his daughter…I just didn't think Millie could handle that. All she thinks is that my life was threatened, and that I've been acting very paranoid since. Jesus. I'm scared. Really scared."

"That's what Janet said. That she was scared."

"She did? Why, I wonder?"

"I don't know. She had a bad dream, I think. She thought she heard something."

And then, like punctuation to what I'd said, something landed heavily, thuddingly, out in the open area of the building, the central shaft area, a *whump* sound with overtones of brittle breaking sounds, like a bag of laundry that had been heaved onto the cement, only somebody had left something breakable in some of the coat and pants pockets, something made of china perhaps, some things that would shatter when hitting the cement…

I held Castile back with an arm, reached over with my free hand and flicked on a small lamp on an end table.

There was a naked body in the center of the floor, out in the open area. Oh, not exactly in the center, maybe, but close. The body was that of a man, and he'd hit face down, but twisting as he did, so that the trunk of him was visible, and there was no mistaking who it was.

Frankie Waddsworth, superstar of porn, wouldn't have to sweat getting it up, anymore.

25

"Jesus," Castile said.

I was kneeling next to the body. Castile was keeping his distance, though he was close enough for us to be able to speak in hushed tones. The only light was from the one lamp in the room where we'd been talking, and it made Castile cast a long, irregular shadow, helping make the already eerie, absurd situation all the more unsettling.

"So much for my nothing's-going-to-happen-tonight theory," I said.

"How can you…touch him?"

I was examining the body.

"Well I'm not getting a kick out of it," I said. "But it's not going to kill me, either."

"You have such a soothing way of putting things," he said.

"Thanks."

I could find no wounds of any kind—bullet or knife or anything else, although if he'd been killed, say, with a long narrow needle or something, the wound wouldn't be readily visible, particularly in this lousy light. One thing was obvious enough: his neck was broken; he'd landed on it, after apparently having fallen the entire four floors.

"Who's sleeping on the upper floor?"

"Just Waddsworth...was. I believe."

"Well he's sleeping downstairs tonight."

"You don't think this is...your Turner's work? Do you?"

"Maybe. Probably. Janet said she heard arguing. Maybe this is the aftermath of a quarrel up at the fag convention upstairs. I don't know."

Castile touched his throat, like he just heard Dracula was in town. "Then Turner could be inside the lodge... right now."

"He could be. Or his partner could've done this. Or Waddsworth could've slipped and fell."

"You don't really believe this could be an accident."

"I don't believe anything except that this sucker's dead as they come, and he could be starting a trend."

"My God."

I stood and joined Castile and we both cast long shadows on Waddsworth.

"We're not telling anybody about this," I said. "Somebody in the lodge already knows, of course...whoever pushed Waddsworth, that is...and that somebody'll expect us to wake everybody up and start hollering and everything. We won't do that."

"We won't?"

"No. We won't do anything that's expected of us. Whoever is responsible for this has thrown me off balance...and I'd like to do the same back at him."

"The poor son of a bitch."

"Who?"

"Waddsworth."

"Oh. Yeah. Sure. Anyway, let's go ahead and search the place and see if we can find Turner."

"Then you *do* think he's in the lodge?"

"He could be. But it's a good idea to batten down the hatches anyway, right? You want to get that gun of yours?"

"All right."

"And tell your wife you're switching rooms. Take another room on the same floor, but get out of that room you're in now."

"What excuse'll I give her?"

"Tell her there's a draft in the room. Tell her anything. But don't tell her about Waddsworth. We'll save that little surprise for morning...if we make it to morning."

"Jesus."

"Go on. Get the gun. We'll search the place together."

He nodded, and headed toward the stairs. He glanced back once, at the naked dead figure sprawled on the rust-color shag carpet, and shuddered and went on.

26

We searched the lodge and didn't find Turner. Of course he could've been hiding in somebody's room, specifically the somebody who was in this with him. But all of the rooms that were supposed to be empty were empty, as was the basement, which was nothing but cement walls and floor and a big furnace.

And so I sent Castile off to bed, to the room he'd moved himself and his wife to, just a few doors down from their old room, which I intended to sleep in. Or rather to not sleep in. To wait in, for Turner and/or somebody else to come dropping in to see Castile.

I had a good idea who that somebody was, too. I hadn't told Castile, as I always like to keep some information to myself, to stay in control of things; but based upon the description Turner had given, under the gun, of his partner Burden ("Short guy, balding, on the heavy side...late forties, early fifties"), Harry the fat cameraman was it.

I'd thought about going after my nine-millimeter, but had decided against it. It would mean going outside, in the dark, and that would be putting myself on a platter for Turner. And I didn't want to go waving a gun around in here: I was, after all, a writer for *Oui* magazine, as far as everybody but Castile was concerned, and it was a cover I didn't want blown. Now that there had been a death there would be a certain amount of investigation by the sheriff's office and it would be very difficult for me to fade into the background of that investigation once I'd gone waving an automatic around. So for the time being, the gun stayed hidden out in the tool chest in the shed.

Since I intended staying awake all night, I shouldn't have any trouble, no matter who came calling. All I had to do was flick on a light before I got mistaken for Castile and killed; it was that simple. If it was Turner, he'd want to find out what the hell I was doing here, before he did anything else; if it was Turner's partner, which is to say Harry, in all probability, he'd be confused seeing someone besides Castile and wife in that particular room, and while he was confused I could either talk or act.

So there was little immediate danger, which is one reason I decided to keep my commitment to Janet to spend the night with her. It was easier keeping my date with her than explaining my way out of it, and gave me the chance to keep a protective eye on her.

So I changed the sheets on the bed and otherwise made the room look like no one had been using it; Castile and his wife had taken their luggage with them, and that helped. It was my hope that Janet wouldn't have paid any special attention to which room the Castiles had been sharing and would think this was simply another vacant room in the big lodge, especially since she'd be somewhat groggy from having already been asleep and wakened to move through the darkness of the place under my direction.

And it worked. I went in and woke her and told her to come with me, and led her into what used to be the Castiles' room and got almost no complaint from her. Almost. She did question me as to why we were moving at all, which I expected her to, since she already had a perfectly good and identical room, as did I, but when I told her I changed because I liked the view, she bought it. There really was a view: the heat in the lodge was working well enough to defrost the windows a bit, and it had stopped snowing out there sometime during my long conversation with Castile, and the temperature was apparently rising somewhat, too.

At any rate, there was a view: the room faced the slope covered with trees, with that winding drive, and the farmhouse at the bottom, over to the left, where I had stowed my car in the barn. Of course I couldn't see the farmhouse, but I could see something that might have been smoke coming from that direction. Smoke coming from the chimney of the farmhouse?

But I didn't look at the view. Not for long. I got in the sack and quickly made what must have seemed like passionate love to Janet, but which was in reality the most paranoid sexual act I have committed since masturbating in an unlocked bathroom in my aunt's house at age thirteen. It's difficult to screw and look over your shoulder at the same time, but that's about what the situation was: at any given moment, somebody might be coming through that unlocked door looking to kill Castile, and here I was in Castile's room, in his bed, screwing instead of paying attention to not getting killed.

Anyway, it made for another memorable lovemaking session with Janet, if not a particularly enjoyable one, though she seemed to like it: it was a frenzied enough act to qualify as the sort of rape-with-permission that some women have a kink for.

"Oh Jack," she said, cuddling to me, as I sat in bed, leaning back against the headboard, staring at the doorway in the near dark (I'd left a light on in the john, left the door open a crack). "I didn't know it could be like this."

"Me either."

"I'm sorry I offended you before."

"Huh?"

"When I accused you of...spying on me...for my father."

"That's okay."

"I really have thought of you. Often. Well. Not often maybe. But I've thought of you."

"I know, Janet."

"I wish..."

"What?"

"I wish we had a chance to get to know each other better."

"Janet, there was the three times that night at my place, and then there was this afternoon, and just now...how much better can we get to know each other, anyway?"

"You're still mad at me. I can tell."

"No. No I'm not."

"Well you seem a little edgy."

"I do at that."

"Otherwise you wouldn't say things like you said."

"What things?"

"Implying our relationship isn't anything but sexual."

"Oh."

"I just don't think you're that kind of person."

"What kind of person is that?"

"Who thinks of a woman…of me…as a mere sex object. The kind of person that this silly film we're making here is made for."

"I thought you liked the film."

"I like working on it. There's a difference."

"Oh."

"I hate the film. But I like working with Castile. He's a real filmmaker, and he'll go on to better things…much better. I'm just being an opportunist, in trying to get in good with him and maybe work on his next film. The one for American International."

"I kind of guessed that."

"You think I'm just a shallow little girl, don't you? An opportunistic little bitch? Maybe I am just a sex object to you…maybe I am just a…cunt."

Her voice was trembling and I had a hunch the tears were not far behind, so I touched her face and said, "Don't say that. It's not true."

And that did the trick. Despite the semi-darkness, her smile was radiant. She snuggled up to me and said, "You can use me as a sex object, if you like. But someday we'll get to know each other better. I just know we will."

Frankly, I wouldn't have minded that at all. She was flaky, yes, but she was as intelligent as she was pretty and was pleasant to be around. There was something appealing about the combination of career girl and sweet kid, opportunist and innocent, and I wouldn't have minded spending some time with her someplace else but here, in this goddamn lodge, a naked corpse downstairs and at least one killer running around the halls out there.

"Can I tell you the truth about something?" she asked.

"Okay."

"You're the first…you know, older guy I ever made it with."

"Older?"

"Yeah, I know…you're only, what? Thirty? But that's still, like, eighty years older than me. I was only twenty when I got out of college, you know. And you're a friend of my father's, so…well that had something to do with why I came onto you, that time. I suppose it was something psychological. Like wanting to get back at my father for treating me like a kid—which he still does to this day—and also like a subconscious desire to sleep with my father, too. Which is a subconscious desire on everybody's part."

"Not mine."

"Well, with you it'd be your mother, I guess. You know what I mean. Don't make fun."

"What you're trying to say is I'm like a father to you. When we're screwing, that is."

She gave me a playful gouge in the ribs. "You're mean."

"And you're a little crazy."

Her smile lit the room up some more. "Do you mind?"

I was smiling, too. For real. "No I don't," I admitted. "I kind of like it."

"Do you think we could get together…later?" she said. "After this is over?"

"I think so. But we won't tell your father."

"Aw, screw him."

"Isn't that what we've been doing?"

And she laughed, and I laughed a little, too, and there was a noise at the door.

I turned on the lamp by the bed, wondering if maybe I shouldn't have gone after my nine-millimeter after all.

Janet said, "What…?"

The door opened.

It was Harry, all right. Just like I thought it would be.

Only he looked strange. He was still wearing the CUBS sweatshirt, but he had no trousers on, just boxer shorts with a loud pattern. He was holding his throat. Red was seeping between his fingers. His eyes were large. His face was pale. He spread his hands and they were smeared with red, garish red, like Technicolor before it was perfected; and now more red was pouring down onto the CUBS shirt, staining it, soaking it, and he was moving his lips. He was trying to speak. He was having trouble.

His throat was cut.

27

"Stop screaming," I said, and Janet stopped screaming.

Harry was on the floor, on his belly, where he'd fallen, arms and legs splayed out, like he was something pinned down for a biology student to dissect. Blood oozed from either side of Harry's head and made the carpet soggy; it was a puke-yellow shag, and Janet was over by the bed adding another layer. I didn't bother bending down to check if Harry was dead or not. With his throat cut ear to ear, Harry wasn't going to be making any miraculous recovery.

Janet had stopped retching now and was sitting on the bed, her face turned away from Harry, and from me as well. Both hands were dug into her hair and she was pulling it, hurting herself, out of some instinct or other, to keep her from going into shock maybe, or perhaps to distract her from what she'd just seen.

A light had gone on out in the hall, shortly after Janet had begun screaming, and now Castile's wife was in the doorway, in her green terry-cloth robe, her hair in curlers, her face white with some facial treatment. She looked a little worse than Harry.

"My God," she said, in a small voice, as she touched a large breast with a medium-size hand. "Is that…"

"Harry," I said.

"What...?"

"His throat's been slashed. Where's your husband?"

"I don't know."

"What?"

"He heard something."

"When? Where?"

"We were in bed...he heard something, he said...out in the hall...five minutes ago...ten minutes ago."

"Shit."

"He has a gun. He was nervous, went out to see what the noise was...with the gun..."

"Shit. We have to find him. Where's that kid Richie? Why didn't Janet screaming get him out of bed, like it did you?"

"I don't know. He must still be in his room."

"Where's that?"

"Couple doors down."

"Let's check on him."

"I...I don't..." Her eyes were staring to take on a glazed look.

"You're coming with me, so snap out of it. You, too, Janet." Janet was sitting on the bed, weeping. "Listen, Mrs. Castile...Millie...your husband's in danger. We all are, but especially him. It's important we find him."

She nodded. She was still in the doorway and I was over by the bed, by Janet. Harry was on the floor between. It wasn't smelling good in there: Harry, like a lot of people, had shit his pants when he died; and then there was the stench from Janet puking.

"Let's get out of here," I said to Janet. She took my hand, and got on her feet, a little wobbly, but on her feet, and she carefully stepped around Harry, like somebody walking through a yard frequented by dogs. She got her jeans and sweater, slipped into them. I'd already made myself decent.

Once we were all in the hallway, Mrs. Castile said, "What about him?" She meant Harry.

"He'll be fine," I said, and closed the door.

And with the door closed, both women seemed relieved, but it didn't last long: Janet soon spotted Waddsworth, doing his *Naked and the Dead* impression down at the bottom of the central shaft area, which this open hallway overlooked.

This time, however, Janet didn't scream: she just pointed, her mouth open, but no words coming out, yet.

Mrs. Castile wasn't reacting at all. Her eyes seemed glazed over again, or maybe she was getting numb. Or maybe she already knew about Waddsworth: maybe Castile hadn't listened to my advice and had told his wife about Waddsworth's fall.

"Is he…" Janet said.

"Yes."

"When did this…happen?"

"Not long after you came down and asked me to come up to bed."

"But you didn't say anything…"

"I didn't want to alarm you. We decided, Castile and I, when it happened, not to go waking everyone up and upsetting them."

"But I was already awake…and we…we were together… when he was…down there, like that…and you…knew…" She shivered and turned away.

"There's no time for that," I said. "Waddsworth's death could be an accident, but not Harry's. I mean, he didn't cut himself shaving. Somebody's in this joint knocking people off, and we've got to get hold of ourselves and deal with that. Got me, Janet? Millie?"

Janet, still facing away, consented to nod.

Mrs. Castile said nothing; she just looked blank, remote in her white face and curlers and green robe, like an extra in a science-fiction film.

But she wasn't entirely gone. When I said, "Lead me to the kid's room. Richie," she did, a room identical to the other bedrooms in the place, and it was empty: the rumpled sheets showed the bed had been used, for something, if not sleeping. But no Richie.

Something else, though.

"Blood," I said, and pointed at a puddle of it near the doorway, sogging up the yellow shag.

"It's out here, too," Janet said, her anger with me making her more coherent, less prone to vomiting and weeping and such. "We've been…walking through it…" And she shivered again.

"Harry got his throat cut here," I said, following the trail of blood Janet had indicated, which led back to where we'd just been. "He staggered down the hall to…"

And I cut that short, because I didn't want to mention that the room Janet and I'd been in had originally been Castile's, as that would mean explaining why we had been in that particular room to both Janet and Mrs. Castile.

Downstairs, a door opened and shut. Noisily. An outside door.

"Who's down there?" I called. Yelled, my voice echoing.

"Me," Castile's voice echoed back, and in a minute he was with us.

He was in the DIRECTOR sweatshirt and jeans, still, and his cheeks were red and his breath heavy.

I told him about Harry and he said, "God, no...I was afraid of something like that," and he asked to have a private word with me, and we moved away from the two women for a moment, and Janet watched us with suspicion. Mrs. Castile looked at the wall.

"I saw him," he said.

"Who?"

"Turner."

"What did you do, go after him?"

"Yes. I heard some noise in the hall, and when I stepped outside the room, I practically bumped into him. Then he ran. Saw my gun, I guess. I went after him, but stumbled on the stairs, and he was outside before I'd even got a real look at him...it was dark in here, no lights on at all... I looked around for him outside, and didn't see him, and finally got a little scared...I mean, I got to thinking that even with a gun, I was out of my league...so I came back in."

"That was very wise. Are you sure it was Turner? Could it have been Richie?"

"It didn't look like Richie."

"Bigger than Richie?"

"I think so. Not Richie. But I didn't really see him. He was just a blur, a shape moving in the hall, running. He'd… just done that to Harry, hadn't he…"

"Maybe. I don't know. Maybe he didn't do it."

"What?"

"Maybe he was just in here to check out the situation, talk to his partner a second. Harry was his partner, you know."

"Harry?"

"I'm pretty sure he was. I think Richie killed Harry. I think it's a case of Harry pushing Waddsworth, and Richie knowing about it, and reacting to it. It's the only way it makes sense to me."

"What do we do now?"

"Richie isn't in his room, so we better see if he's anywhere in the lodge. Fuck. This is getting out of hand. I don't like this at all."

"What do we do when we find Richie?"

"We'll worry about that when we find him. Here. Give me that gun."

He did. It was a nickel-plated snub-nose .38.

"Ladies," I said, going over to where they were standing. "We're about to have a tour of the premises. Stem to stern. Stay close together at all times."

Janet had a look of anger on her face, mixed in with confusion, and both reactions were justified; but she went along on the search without a word of complaint.

Which was also true of Mrs. Castile, who allowed her husband to guide her by the arm, but she was going deeper and deeper into herself, into an almost catatonic state.

The search of the lodge took twenty minutes. Nobody home but us.

No Richie. No Turner.

Just Castile and his wife, Janet and me, and of course Waddsworth and Harry.

And then, later than I should've, I noticed something about the gun: it seemed light. I'd never used a nickel-plated gun in my life, and rarely used a revolver of any kind, so it took me a while to pick up on it, but just as we'd finished searching the basement, the last and most unsettling stop on our tour, I noticed the gun being light and examined it and said, with some irritation, "Castile… there aren't any bullets in this fucking thing."

"What?"

"Bullets. Those little lead things that come flying out when you squeeze the trigger, remember?"

"Let me see it."

I broke the gun open and showed him.

"It *was* loaded," he said. With a little desperation. "There's a box of ammunition upstairs, in one of my suit-cases."

"Let's get it."

We went up to the room he and his wife had recently moved to, and the box of slugs was not there: not in his suitcase, not anywhere.

"Gone," he said: "Someone...got in here and unloaded the gun, and took the bullets. Jesus!"

Enough of this bullshit. Time to go out to the shed and get the nine-millimeter.

"Castile," I said, "you and your wife stay here. Janet and I are going outside for a while."

Castile nodded.

"No," Janet said.

"We're safer paired off," I said. "You're coming with me."

"I...I'll need my jacket...and my glasses..."

"Okay."

"My jacket's in the front closet, but..."

"But what?"

"My glasses are...are...in with Harry."

"I'll get them for you."

And I did, and we got our jackets from the front closet and went outside.

28

It was still cold, but the wind had died. Now, instead of pushing you around, the cold air was settling for cutting through you. Still, it was not an entirely unpleasant sensation, not unlike a splash of water in the face in the morning, waking you up, getting you alert, giving clarity to things.

The sky was clear now, and stars were out, and the moon, illuminating the white landscape, making the snow glitter in places where the light reflected, giving the grounds of the lodge an aura of peaceful unreality, which was a little disconcerting at the moment.

Janet huddled close to me, hanging onto my arm like she expected the law of gravity to be revoked any time now. She'd apparently forgotten about being pissed off at me and was concentrating on being scared. She'd glance up at me every few seconds, her eyes somewhat vague behind fogged-up glasses, but there was affection and something resembling trust in the looks she gave me, and I found that oddly reassuring. I liked her. Everybody else around here was weird or dead or both. She was just a little crazy, and pleasantly so. She didn't belong here.

Me either, but that was beside the point. I was here, and Janet too, and so, it would seem, was Turner. I could only think of two possible scenarios for what had been going on here. First, as I'd suggested to Castile, Turner might've come in to talk to Harry, his partner, about the final details of the coming hit, and instead had found Waddsworth dead and possibly his partner the same way, and Turner, like any pro who wandered into a situation like that, would have turned tail and run, which is precisely what he seemed to have done, according to Castile. Or second, perhaps Turner had in fact killed Harry, out of displeasure over Harry getting involved in that Gay Lib love triangle and killing Waddsworth and messing up the contracted-for job; and this made a kind of sense, because once Waddsworth had died, a sheriff's investigation was a foregone conclusion, and Turner might not have wanted to leave a live partner behind, to talk to the authorities and play plea-bargaining games and eventually involve Turner himself.

While the latter explanation was marginally possible, I just couldn't see Turner using a knife or razor or whatever and cutting somebody's throat. Too messy. Just not professional at all. I'd seen the tool of Turner's trade back in his room at Wilma's: that Browning automatic with the silencer built in by a gunsmith. And I was not entirely satisfied with the first scenario, either, as it seemed unlikely to me Turner would come into the house prior to actually making the hit. His telephone communications cut off, Turner would signal his partner somehow and then meet him outside for a talk...but inside the lodge? Didn't make sense.

Neither did the tracks in the snow.

The snow had drifted and in places didn't come up over my shoes and in other places was up to my waist and to Janet's boobs. Over in the parking lot the snow-heavy cars were strange shapes amidst rolling drifts of white, while the stretch of ground between the lodge and its tool shed was barely a foot deep. And that was where the set of tracks was visible, two pairs of overlapping footprints leading away from the lodge, another set, a single pair of footprints, leading back. The tracks headed toward the shed but stopped about halfway, where someone had apparently fallen; then a smooth path had been made from that point on, as if by a sled, right up to the double doors of the shed.

Janet and I studied the tracks in silence for a while, then exchanged puzzled looks, and I said, "I'm going in there and have a look."

"What do I do?"

"Wait here."

"What…what if somebody's in there?"

"Then somebody besides me may come out."

"What do I do then?"

"Make a run for it, wouldn't be a bad idea."

"You're joking."

"Yeah. Right. Me and Waddsworth and Harry'll all have a laugh about it in the showers after the game."

"Where…where would I run to?"

"I don't know. Improvise. Down into the woods would be best. You're just going to have to fend for yourself."

"You're a real comfort."

"I'm going to work hard at not getting killed in there. That's the best I got to offer you."

"Jack..."

"What?"

"I'm just scared, that's all. Shook up, is all. Jack."

"What?"

"Nothing. Go ahead. Go in your goddamn shed, will you?"

I walked toward the shed. The panel truck parked against it was engulfed in a drift and any thought I might've had about somebody hiding in the truck was immediately discarded. As I walked I checked my pockets for possible weapons. At one point I'd had wire cutters, but I'd tossed them away, after snipping the phone wires; I'd had a screwdriver, too, which I left in the shed. Terrific. Well, I had my car keys, and I slid each of three keys between my knuckles so that the jagged-edged little pieces of metal extended from the fist that seemed to be the only weapon I had on me.

I kicked the door open. Why fuck around. And I threw myself in, like you'd throw something down off a truck you were helping unload. The snowmobile stopped me. It's what I knocked into, and bounced off of, rolling over against the wall and by that time I'd seen that Turner wasn't in there, and neither was anybody else.

I put my car keys away.

Someone *had* been in here: apparently whoever it was had tried to start the snowmobile, because the tarp was off and lay bubbled over against the far wall.

I bent over the trunk-like tool chest and opened it and dug down, looking for the nine-millimeter. I came up immediately with the silencer, which I had detached and hidden in there separately, and kept digging and came rapidly to the conclusion that I wasn't going to find it.

The nine-millimeter was gone.

I stood and indulged in a long sigh and went over and checked the other tool chest, the one with the garden tools, where I'd hidden the rotors from the cars, and checked the jar of nails, where I'd put the sparkplugs from the snowmobile and snowplow and everything was where I put it.

Just that one thing missing: the gun.

Like I told Janet, sometimes you have to improvise, so I dug back around in the tool chest and found a small crowbar, which was certainly a better makeshift weapon than my fist and some car keys, and as I was doing that, I noticed a red puddle over by the canvas tarp that had been flung against the wall, by whoever tried to start the snowmobile.

So I went over and lifted the tarp off the floor to see where the red puddle had come from and found the answer.

Richie.

29

Castile met us at the door.

"Where's your wife?" I said, stepping inside.

"She was tired, " he said. "Had a headache, wanted to be by herself a while."

"I told you to stay together."

"You didn't say that."

"I said it."

"We just searched the lodge, remember? There's nobody in here but us."

Janet was huddling behind me. Shivering.

"What's wrong with her?" Castile said.

"She didn't like what I just told her," I said.

"What did you tell her?"

"That I saw Richie in the shed."

"What's he doing there?"

"Not much. He's under a tarp with his throat cut. Ear to ear. Like a great big smile."

"Jesus," Castile said.

"Take me up to your wife."

"She's resting, I said."

"Take me up there. Now."

"Okay," he said, and turned to lead the way. I hit him in the back with the crowbar.

30

A few minutes shy of two hours later, Castile woke up. He was sitting, tied to a straight-back chair, in the sunken living room in front of the fireplace, on the fake fur rug where, not so long ago, his wife and Frankie Waddsworth had humped for the cameras. Even now the massive black camera, a boom mike, the lights on tripods, looked silently on.

"What…Jesus…what's going…"

He tried to move and couldn't and looked down at himself and saw the thick rubberized cable I'd used to tie him to the chair and when he saw it, going around his chest perhaps twenty times, and then down around his legs and through the rungs of the chairs, he knew there was no reason to try to budge.

"Good morning," I said.

"What the fuck are you doing to me?"

"It's almost dawn."

"Where's my wife?"

"You know where you wife is. She's upstairs with her throat slashed. Where you left her."

"This is a mistake…"

"Right. Anyway, we're alone in the place, Castile. I sent Janet away. Of course we're not exactly alone…

there's Waddsworth over there, and Harry's upstairs, and Richie's outside…and then there's your wife…"

His face became slack. His body too. It was like he was a figure molded in clay that was starting to lose shape. His red hair, once so carefully groomed by his ex-hairdresser wife to disguise that it was thinning, looked wilted now.

"I…I guess there isn't much point in…pretending I don't understand what you're saying…"

"I guess not," I said.

He could see the nine-millimeter in my gloved hand. I'd found the gun upstairs, in one of the built-in bureaus in one of the unused bedrooms on the fourth floor.

He got a weary smile going. "And now what…you kill me?"

"No."

"Then, what? Oh. You…you figure to…leave me here, and this Turner will come along and finish his job."

"Turner's not going to kill you. He's going to come in here in a while and take one look at any one of the dead bodies you've accumulated and he's going to get his ass out. First rule of the profession is if anything's out of whack, if things aren't going exactly according to plan, then fuck it. Get out. And he will. So you aren't in any danger from him, if I should decide to just leave you here."

"You…you'd do that? Just leave me here, and go?"

"I might."

"What do you want for it…money? I told you before… I can get you money. Eight thousand, we were talking…I could get you that, I could get you more…"

"That's not what I want from you."

"Then what…what *do* you want?"

"I want what happened…and I want it here." And I tapped the big tape recorder I'd brought over from the table by the wall, where Janet had sat and done the sound on the film.

"I don't understand."

"You're going to tell the whole story. Beginning with the phone call you got from that guy whose daughter starred in the snuff flick. I want it all…everything…with one exception. You're going to leave me out of it. And Janet too. I was never here. And Janet left here, before the storm set in…well before the shit started hitting the fan."

"And you want this…on tape?" He was looking at me like he thought I was crazy. It didn't bother me. His opinion didn't mean a whole lot to me.

"I want it on tape," I said "I know your intention was to throw the blame for what you did my way…you figured, and rightly, that if I was around for an investigation to focus on, you'd be in the clear. Once they had hold of me and dug into who I am and what I've done, I'd be a natural for the leading role in this little horror movie you've been stage-managing. So my way around that is simple: I was never here. When they find you here, you can tell any story you like…anything you can come up with that'll save your ass…but just make sure I'm not a part of that story, and that Janet has a bit part. Because I'm going to have your story on tape…the story of what really happened here…to use against you if you ever try to implicate me. So I won't have to worry. Janet, either."

He considered that for a moment, and then he tried out a small smile. "If I don't make your tape…if I tell you to go fuck yourself…what then?"

"I'll think of something," I said, and I got the straight razor out of my pocket. I'd found it on him, when I patted him down after knocking him out with the crowbar. I flipped it open, the razor swinging out of its white plastic handle. The edge caught some light and winked. The surface of it wasn't entirely clean, however: there were still flecks of something on it, brown flecks that had been red.

"All right," he said. "And if I do make the tape…?"

I tucked the razor back in its plastic handle and put it in my pocket. "I'll leave you here."

"Tied up like this?"

"Yes. That's to your benefit. If you're tied up and everybody else in the house is dead, when you're found, then obviously somebody else was here. So you can pin the blame on that imaginary somebody."

"Why would a killer kill everybody else in the house, and leave me alive?"

"I'll toss you behind that couch over there. You can say the killer forgot about you. Lost count."

"That's stupid."

"Not really. When Richard Speck killed those nurses in Chicago, he lost count. One of them hid under the bed and got out alive. They'll buy it. Leave it to them to come up with the explanation."

"Maybe it would work…"

"It will. Now. I'm going to turn on the tape recorder, and once it's going, I won't be talking anymore. This is your show. Make it good."

And I hit the switch.

31

He began where I told him to, with the midnight phone call and snuff flicks and how he'd been living in fear for the past six months, getting little sleep that whole time, and when he did sleep he had cold-sweat-variety nightmares, and when he was awake he thought about the nightmares he'd been having, and took to carrying a gun with him and just generally jumping every time he heard a noise and sometimes when he didn't.

He described briefly the filming of the porno flick here at the lodge, how the first fleet of actors had left the day before, and how Janet Stein had left in the afternoon, just before the rest of them got snowed in, and then he went into Waddsworth's fall, and how he, Castile, had reacted to it.

"I was sure he'd been murdered," Castile said, "by whoever it was that'd been hired to murder me. I just... *knew*...that the paid killer that Meyers had hired was in this lodge...to kill me...maybe to kill everyone in the lodge, now that we were snowbound...and my wife, when I went back to my room and told her, about Waddsworth's death, and what I thought it could mean, she tried to convince me it could've been an accident, or the result of an argument between those three faggots upstairs...but I couldn't buy it. I *knew*...after all those paranoid months...that this was it...that the attempt would be made tonight.

"Of the four of us left in the lodge..." And here he paused to give me a look, emphasizing that he had left Janet and me out, in his tally of the number of people present. "...my wife and I made two, and that left only Harry Belcher, a cameraman from Chicago, and his young 'friend' Richie Hudson. Harry was the older man, the more physically tough of the two, Richie being an ineffectual type...so obviously Harry seemed the more likely of the two, to make a living by violence. Another possibility was that the two men were in on it together...they lived together, lovers is what they were...perhaps they were in business, too, or at least knew each other's business.

"So I made an excuse to my wife, about hearing a noise in the hall, and I took my gun and went to Harry's room. He was in bed...Richie wasn't there...Richie had his own room, but that had been for appearance's sake, and I'd expected them to be together...had been ready to confront the both of them, threaten them with the gun, make them tell me, make them *admit* who they really were...or anyway who Harry was...I wasn't completely convinced that little fag Richie was a part of it, though I couldn't risk taking a chance he wasn't.

"He...Harry...was sitting on the side of his bed...lights on...he was holding his head in his hands. He looked up at me, and I showed him the gun, and didn't have a word out before he'd jumped at me.

"It wasn't supposed to go like that…I was supposed to hold the gun on him and he would tell what I needed to hear and then…I don't know what…then, maybe, I would have killed him. I hadn't thought it through that far…I was just acting out of reflex, doing what I thought I needed to survive.

"And now, Jesus! I was fighting. A man so much stronger than me it was ridiculous…if he'd thought to hit me, just use his fist on me, he'd have had me. But he didn't. We just sort of wrestled. He was concentrating on the gun I had…trying to twist it out my hand…so we wrestled, rolled around on the floor like a couple of kids rough-housing.

"That's when Richie came in. He must've been next door, or maybe he was off alone someplace pouting about what happened to Waddsworth…but anyway he came in, and made a sound, like he'd been hit in the stomach, air rushing out…I could see him out of the corner of my eye, standing there waving his arms in the air, like he'd spotted somebody drowning and he didn't know how to swim and couldn't do anything about it…and then he sort of ran off, toward the bathroom and he came back with the straight razor.

"He stood over us, Harry and me, and in a shaky voice told me to drop the gun. Somehow that struck me funny, not that I took time to laugh about it, but here was this skinny little faggot spouting a cliched line out of an old western: 'Drop the gun.' It just seemed absurd to me. The whole thing seemed absurd.

"But of course I did as he said. And Harry let up on me, stood away from me, and I got up from off the floor, but as I did, I kicked out, at Richie's legs, and there was a sort of a struggle, just me and Richie this time, while Harry looked on helplessly, and I ended up with the razor.

"Harry was almost to where I'd dropped the gun…he almost had time to pick it up…but he saw me…he saw the razor…and didn't do it. He just backed up. They both backed up. And this weird thing happened…this kind of surge went through me. All the wrestling, scuffling…that sort of thing isn't like anything I'd ever be involved with… but it had me confused…it also…I was, in a weird way, excited by it, and I did something that had no thinking to it at all: I lunged at Harry, like a fucking lion-tamer, and he backed up some more, toward the doorway…and he almost lost his footing, but not quite, not even when I lashed out with the razor and caught him across the throat…he just sort of reached up and touched where he'd been cut, with both his hands, and stumbled out of there, walking somehow, don't ask me how.…

"And Richie, Richie was running…I don't know why he didn't scream. Maybe he was too scared to…but he ran, ran down the stairs, out of the house, and I caught him outside, and he was crying, just blubbering, and he made me mad, for some reason, he just made me mad, made my head throb for a second, and my face felt hot, cold as it was out there, and me not in a coat…and suddenly I was…it was happening, but I was watching it happen. I was detached, somehow, distant and close at the same time, doing and watching, and you know something funny? I didn't get any blood on me…not when I lashed out and cut Harry, not when I took Richie in the shed and cut his throat. There was a lot of blood, but none of it got on me…not until my wife."

And here he paused again and his eyes were watery and his voice was wavery, like poor TV reception.

"She put up with a lot from me, Millie did. She did a lot for me. She even stayed by me, when she found out about those snuff things I handled…the idea of them, it sickened her. She was really…very sensitive. She wasn't tough enough for this business…she…you have to be willing to do whatever you have to."

He stopped. He began to cry. He didn't make any noise as he did; that part he held in. But the tears flowed, and after a while I kicked him a little and he went on.

"She gave me money…financed me, my career…it was all her doing. She fucked people on the screen, for me, because I asked her to. She'd do anything for me. She believed in me. She wasn't any angel…I mean, she was in it for herself, too…wanted a career in aboveground movies, wanted to be a real star…and that was going to be a problem for me. I needed to leave all my ties to the porno industry behind, and she was going to be something of an embarrassment, expecting parts in the post-porno films I'd make. She knew things about me…about things I'd done, to get ahead in the business…the snuff films, for instance…that meant I couldn't get her out of my life, a divorce was out of the question. Very soon our marriage would've turned into a sort of blackmail situation...she was capable of that. Still...I liked her. I did. She was important to me...do anything for me...but this... this was too much...she couldn't couldn't...I couldn't..."

He stopped again. Took in a couple breaths. He wasn't crying anymore.

"She knew I'd killed Harry. It wasn't hard for her to figure out. She told me she knew. I didn't deny it. I told what I'd done and I told her about Richie. I said I was sorry but that it had just...happened...that things had just...got out of hand. She just looked at me. I told her no one would ever have to know I'd done it...we could cover it up somehow, I said, I knew we could...

"And she started beating on me with her fists. She'd been very quiet till then, that surface calm that hysteria hides behind sometimes, and she just...attacked me, but she was saying things, not screaming, almost whispering... not this, she said, not murder, not that...and she said... this is exactly what she said, hitting me...she said, I can't live with that.

"The razor was in my hand and I grabbed her by the hair and pulled her head back and her eyes were...they were sad...not full of pain or anger or hatred or anything...they were sad...and I cut her throat.

"This time there was blood. On my hands. On my arms. I went into the bathroom and I washed my hands."

He smiled. The practiced smile I'd seen so much of lately.

"It's like I told Millie," he said. "It just got out of hand… things just started happening…quickly…it was like somebody else was doing those things…it was unreal…like the movies."

And then he laughed at what he'd just said, and the laughter turned into a racking sound and when he stopped making the racking sound, his head hung loose above the DIRECTOR shirt, his body slack again, the cables holding him in like a man in an electric chair that's done its work already.

I switched off the recorder.

"That's all I need," I said.

"Tell me…" he said, coming back to life a little. "Tell me something, Murphy, or whoever the fuck you are… how did you put this together so fast? How did you know it wasn't your Turner who killed Harry and Richie and Waddsworth?"

"Harry probably killed Waddsworth," I said. "But there's no way to know for sure. Not with all three of them dead."

"You mean…it was an argument…love triangle thing…"

"I'm sure of it. But whether Harry freaked and murdered Waddsworth or whether it was accidental, just a fight that got out of control…no one will ever know. Janet heard them arguing, remember, and that's as close to the truth as we'll come."

"What about the rest of it? How did you pick up on me?"

I shrugged. "It was obvious enough what had happened outside, out in the snow. You told me you'd seen Turner in the hall, that it was Turner you'd chased out there…

but the footprints outside told a different story than yours of going out and looking around for Turner and seeing nothing and getting scared and coming back in. There were two sets of prints ending in a smoothed-out area, where you pulled Richie down and struggled a little, then a long smooth trail where you dragged him unconscious to the shed, and then one set of footprints going back to the house."

"And based on that, you came in and hit me with whatever it was you hit me with?"

"It was a crowbar. No. When I looked in the tool chest for my gun and it wasn't there, I knew it was you had taken it. You were the only person who knew I even had a gun. I told you I hid it outside...you were smart enough to know that that meant in the shed. You took a quick look and turned it up, after you finished with Richie...or maybe you went out and found it earlier. Doesn't matter. Either way, could only have been you."

"It could've been Turner who found the gun."

"Why would he be looking for it? Besides, there was a silencer for the gun, in the tool chest, too...I'd hidden it in there, loose. You left it behind. You probably didn't know what the hell it was. Turner, obviously, would've."

"Still...Turner might've been doing all the things I did...I don't see how you knew..."

"Turner has a silenced gun. He wouldn't go around making noises with a straight razor. Besides, I asked him."

"What?"

"Turner was down in that farmhouse, at the bottom of

the hill. I saw smoke from its chimney earlier tonight. My car was hidden in the barn, and while you were tied in the chair, sleeping it off, I took Janet down there and had her stay in the barn while I went in the house to talk to Turner. He was asleep. I woke him up.

"He was surprised to see me. Didn't know I was anywhere around. And that was enough to tell me he wasn't running around doing things at the lodge, which I didn't think he was, anyway. He's dead now."

"He's…you *killed* him? Why?"

"There was a woman named Wilma. I liked her. You've eaten at her place yourself…you mentioned it, remember? I value few people in this life…but she was one. He killed her. And in doing that, he was being careless. Careless about me…I lived almost next door, and had been in the place shortly before Wilma's death, and his doing that could…still could…cause me trouble. He was always doing thoughtless fucking things like that. He almost got me killed once. I didn't like him. And now this. You see, people in Turner's business…the business I used to be in, and still am, marginally…don't go around carelessly destroying life. To you murder's a hobby…Turner was in business. In my way of thinking, that's what separates me from the psychopaths like you. But that's just a rationalization, so the hell with it. Anyway, Turner was careless…he killed Wilma as thoughtlessly, as casually, as he'd humped her sixteen-year-old niece, and…well. What am I doing boring you for? There's no reason for you to have to listen to all this."

I switched the tape recorder back on, took his nickel-plated .38 out of my belt—I'd loaded the gun with ammunition I'd found upstairs, with my nine-millimeter—and swung the gun up toward him. Some light reflected off the shiny barrel as he opened his mouth to say no and I slid the barrel in and squeezed the trigger.

The chair went over backwards with him. Some of what used to be inside his head spattered against the brown brick fireplace and clung.

At this point the tape ran out and began flapping in the machine. I untied the cable from the chair and him and returned the cable to the rest of the black coils of cable and wire covering the area surrounding the movie set like an underbrush. The gun was still in his mouth. I moved his right arm up towards his face and made the fingers touch the gun. The straight razor I put in his pocket.

I almost tripped over Waddsworth on my way out.

32

The first weekend in June I had some men over to play poker. One of them was Bob Katz. He was the last to arrive; the other three men and I were already playing when he got there.

I got up and met him at the door. He was an intense little dark-haired man with glasses; he never seemed entirely at ease in sports clothes, like the red short-sleeve Ban-Lon and plaid bermuda shorts he was wearing now.

Before he'd stepped in the door, he said, "My daughter's down for the weekend. She dropped me off. I'll catch a ride home with one of the others."

"Fine," I said.

"She's waiting out there. Wants to say hello." And he gave me a funny look, like he'd just figured out it hadn't been so wise, that time, to entrust his daughter's honor to me for an evening.

So I sent him over to the big round table I'd set up in the living room, and went outside.

It was a cool night. Overcast. No stars, no moon, for the lake to reflect: just the various color lights from the cottages and the few restaurants and such around the lake.

There's a gravelled area alongside the A-frame, and Bob Katz's big green Lincoln was pulled up there, parked, and Janet was standing by it—not leaning, standing—looking out at the lake.

"Hello," I said.

"Hello Jack," she said. She was in a dark blue halter top with denims, a yellow scarf around her neck. She was pretty as ever, the brown arcs of hair framing her face, her glasses resting on top of her head, pushed up there, like she wanted to look out at the lake and see it through a soft-focus lens. Or maybe it was me she wanted to see that way.

I hadn't seen her since I'd driven her back to Chicago, after we'd spent half the day in that barn, in my GT, waiting for the snowplows to come along and clear the way. She'd huddled with me in the car, and it had been cold, because I hadn't been able to turn on the heat, for fear of carbon monoxide poisoning in the enclosed barn.

But that was then. This was now.

"I hope you don't mind," she said. Her near-baritone voice was soft sounding. Gentle.

"Mind what?"

"My seeing you. You advised against it, remember?"

"Well, it's been two months, practically. It's okay. No one's come round to talk to me about it. You?"

"Yes," she said, looking out at the lake, not me. "They tracked me down…despite my having used Stein instead of Katz as my last name."

"Through your friend at the Playboy Club at Geneva?"

"Right. The one who recommended me to Castile for doing sound. Anyway. Some men came around. It was in

Chicago, and they were Chicago police detectives. I don't know why they were involved...but they were who did the questioning. They were no problem. They talked to me at my apartment a couple of times. That was it."

"What did they ask you?"

"They asked when I'd left the lodge, and I told them in the afternoon before the snow got heavy. Like you suggested. They asked how I got to and from the lodge, and I said I'd taken my car...which I hadn't...Castile had those two men, Harry and Richie, come pick me up...and you drove me home, of course. But the detectives accepted everything I said. They were also good about keeping my real name out of the papers. My parents still don't know I was involved."

"That's good."

"I'm a little numb about it all, to this day. Did you read Castile's confession in the papers? The crazy suicide note he left, on tape? Weird."

"Very."

"That's one of the things the detectives wanted to know about."

"Pardon?"

"The tape Castile made...he didn't say anything about that one man he killed. The detectives showed me pictures of the man and I'd never seen him before...he wasn't anybody who was at the lodge when we were."

"Isn't that strange."

"Yes. They found him in that farmhouse...gives me the creeps just thinking about it. All that time we were sitting in your car, in that barn, cuddling together keeping warm, trying to hold each other a little and forget about some of the ugliness…all that time that man was in that farmhouse, next door, with his throat cut."

"Really."

"It gives me the creeps just thinking about it."

"Don't think about it."

"How could anyone do a thing like that?"

"I don't know."

"I read where the film is going to be released. Isn't that…sick? Just awful?"

"It'll make money."

"I know. I know it will and it's just sick. Oh…I'm sorry. I forgot that you invested in the picture…"

I had told her, in the barn, when she finally got around to asking me whether or not I really was a writer for *Oui* and if not what had I been doing there, that I was a silent partner in the film, that I had invested with Castile and wanted to come around and watch the filming, without announcing myself as one of the "money men."

"I won't be able to come forward for any of the money," I said. "I used a false name and I don't want to stir the investigation up, where I'm concerned."

"That's too bad, in a way. Money is money, after all."

"I guess so."

"Anyway. I just wanted to stop and tell you how things came out on my end…and see how you were doing."

"I'm doing fine."

"I wish it had been different. Not just for those people

that got murdered. You know, it's really something... people are talking about what happened at the lodge in terms of what Manson did and terrible crimes like that... they'll be writing books about it, trying to figure out what exactly went on at that place."

"Good luck to them."

"But I started to say...I wish it could've been different. For us. I think I said back at that lodge...and I know I said it waiting in that car in that barn with you... but I'll say it again: I wish we could get to know each other better, under better circumstances, than either of the times we got thrown together...that first time by my father, the second time, horrible time, at the lodge....But now we never will, I suppose."

"I suppose."

"Every time I'd see you I'd be reminded of what happened back there...and the memory of that is hard enough to deal with without being reminded of it constantly."

"I understand."

"I'm sorry."

"I am too."

She touched my face and got in the Lincoln and pushed her glasses back down and drove away.

I stood there a while, looking out at the lake. There was a breeze. It was cold for June.

I went back to my game.

THE
END

Afterword

Quarry's Cut was originally published by Berkley Books in 1977 as *The Slasher*. The title was my own, though designed to follow a pattern established by an editor who had published my novel *Quarry* as *The Broker*. This has happened to me several times—the first book or two in a series getting retitled by editors, me striving to provide subsequent titles in a similar cadence. I'm sure a lot of mystery writers have gone down this road.

The novel's movie background—porno though it is—reflects my abiding interest in film, but I had not at this stage worked on any films. Recently, in *Quarry's Ex*, I again used the making of a film as the backdrop for a Quarry yarn, and that novel does reflect my experiences. This one just reflects, I'm afraid, that in my twenties I was interested in pornography.

When Foul Play Press republished the first four Quarry novels, my original title for the initial book was restored to *Quarry* and we changed the titles of the other three, as well. I was anxious to change *The Slasher* because another mystery writer called Collins (Michael Collins, a pseudonym of Dennis Lynds) had published a novel of the same name a year or so later. Because I was then publishing as

"Max Collins," the two *Slasher* novels by "M. Collins" began getting confused by libraries and in bibliographic sources. The damn books even had similar covers.

Since Dennis's Michael Collins byline was well established, I decided to begin using my middle name to set me apart from that other Collins. (Dennis once asked me to change my byline, because he felt he had a lock on Collins; I said, "Fine—I'll start using 'Dennis Lynds.' " Nothing more was said on the subject.)

Anyway, anyone out there who figures I use "Max Allan Collins" because I'm a pretentious idiot needs to at least strike "pretentious." You have to be a masochist to use "Allan" as part of a byline, since it's doomed to be misspelled—if they aren't going to get "Edgar Allan Poe" right, what chance do I have?

This was the final of the first four Quarry novels, and it is the darkest, and the most darkly comic, of that quartet. The problem with writing Quarry is that there is a temptation to escalate the nasty things of which he is capable into unpleasantness or absurdity or, for that matter, unpleasant absurdity. I felt I skated near the edge on this one, and perhaps it was good that I did not write another four or fourteen Quarry novels at this stage in my career. I am proud of what I did with the mid-'80s Quarry and the new Quarry novels written for Hard Case Crime, and feel I benefitted, artistically at least, from the long break between books.

Not that I'm apologizing for *Quarry's Cut*. I like black comedy, and I love the freedom of doing whatever sick, twisted thing comes into my mind. My late mentor Don Westlake said that Richard Stark was Westlake getting up on the wrong side of the bed on a rainy day. Quarry is me when I slept on the floor and woke to a thunderstorm.

MAX ALLAN COLLINS

WANT MORE QUARRY?

Try These Other Quarry Novels From
MAX ALLAN COLLINS *and*
HARD CASE CRIME

Quarry

When a job goes horribly wrong, Quarry sets out to find out who hired him—and take revenge.

Quarry's List

When a rival sets out to take over the murder-for-pay business, Quarry finds himself in the crosshairs.

Quarry's Deal

Quarry's plan to target other hitmen for elimination hits a snag when he comes up against a deadly female assassin.

Quarry's Vote

Happily retired, Quarry turns down a million dollars to assassinate a presidential candidate. But it's not the sort of job you can just walk away from…

Read On for the
Opening Chapters of
QUARRY'S VOTE!

I

My big mistake was allowing happiness to creep in.

It's worse than complacency; or maybe it's just the same goddamn thing. But for somebody like me, for somebody with my sort of past, allowing the present to lull you into happy complacency is the surest fucking way to insure you'll have no future at all.

I met Linda when she was vacationing up at Lake Geneva, just another cute blonde among many cute college girls, many of them blond. She wore white—a white tank top that made her seem flat-chested (which she wasn't, really) and white cut-off jeans, cut so short that the lower moons of her cute little ass showed through fringe of the cut-offs. She had china-blue eyes and short, very curly, white-blond hair, a tiny nose and the whitest teeth you ever saw; when she smiled, it was Dimples City —and you just had to like her. Or anyway I did.

I lived, at the time, in an A-frame cottage on Paradise Lake, a small, private lake with a scattering of summer homes. Paradise Lake held no truck with tourists, other than those visiting relatives in one of the cottages, and it afforded me plenty of peace, quiet and privacy. Nearby Lake Geneva, on the other hand, provided plenty of pussy, to put it bluntly, and when I first met Linda that was all she meant to me.

Maybe she made a little more impact on me than the average college girl I'd pick up, in those days; she was, after all, very innocent, or as innocent as a girl can be who goes to bed with you the day you met her. She wasn't terribly sexually experienced, and her idea of being daring was to smoke a little dope. She didn't strike me as terribly bright, but she was funny and cute and when she called me on the phone three months later, I remembered her almost immediately.

"Jack," she said. "This is Linda. Remember me?"

"Sure," I said, unsurely.

"You know. *Linda.*"

And the inflection in her voice brought her back to me.

"Well, Linda. Where are you calling from?"

"H-home."

The catch in her voice, and the static on the line, sent me a message.

"What's wrong?" I asked. "And where is home, anyway?"

"Home is Indiana."

As in back home again in.

"Okay," I said. "Now tell me what the trouble is."

"My folks. They're…"

And I could hear her crying.

"Linda, what is it?" I tried to be sympathetic, fighting irritation.

"My folks were killed last week."

"I'm sorry. What do you mean, killed?" That word

meant something different to me than it might to some people.

"Automobile accident." She swallowed. "New Year's Eve."

It was the first week of January. Linda's parents were just another statistic.

"I'm sorry, kid," I said, trying to mean it, wondering why the hell she was calling me.

"Funeral was a few days ago," she said.

"Yes?" What did this have to do with me?

"I need to get away for a while," she said, in a rush. "I wondered...I wondered if I could come up and spend a few days with you?"

"Well..."

I mean, Christ, she was just some one-night stand. What the hell was this about? That was all I needed, was some college girl moping around my place for a week.

"I don't have anybody, Jack. *Any*-body. My friends are all back at school. My folks were all I had, except for my brother, and he headed back to San Francisco this morning. Now I'm all alone in this house and I don't have anywhere to go."

"Well, uh...go back to college with your friends, why don't you? Best thing in the world for you would be get back in the swing of things."

She paused. Then: "I flunked out. I'm not going back this semester."

She began crying some more.

I'm not particularly soft-hearted, but I remembered

her being a good kid, and who knew? Comforting her might add up to my getting laid regular for a week or so. Would that be so bad?

"You can come stay with me, kid," I said. "Long as you need to."

"Oh, Jack...Jack, I *knew* I could depend on you!"

Why?

"Why don't you fly into Chicago," I said, "and I'll pick you up. At O'Hare."

We'd made the arrangements, and she came and stayed with me for a week. Pretty soon the week turned into a month, and a year later, in a little chapel at Twin Lakes, I married the girl.

Here's the deal. I was thirty-five. I was getting bored with one-night stands and my own microwave cooking. I wanted some company, and she seemed pleasant enough. She talked too much, but most people do. She was beautiful, a terrific cook, and she kept out of my way. What more could I ask?

For many years the notion of living with one woman was out of the question for me. I was in the wrong business to accommodate what Donahue and the women's magazines would refer to as a "relationship." But that business was behind me. I had retired, after socking away a hell of a nest egg. I could live off my investments, one of which was an oddball business called Wilma's Welcome Inn which was just five minutes from my A-frame.

The Welcome Inn was a rambling two-story affair left over from another era—gas station, restaurant, convenience store, and hotel sharing one somewhat ramshackle roof. It struck some chord in me, reminded me of something from my childhood, a place I'd gone with my parents I think. Anyway, I liked the place, for no good reason, and I also liked the gal who ran the place, Wilma.

But Wilma—a nice fat woman who made great chili—died a few years ago, leaving the place in the unsteady hands of her boyfriend/bartender Charley. He was having trouble keeping the business afloat without his porky pillar, and Wilma's niece, a zaftig babe in her late teens who wanted nothing to do with the business except for any money it generated, was not happy with Charley letting things slip; she was threatening to can the ex-con and sell the joint. So I bought it from the girl (who used the dough to stake herself to a move out to California, where she planned to break into the movies—right) and kept Charley on.

When I was a kid back in Ohio, I tinkered around with cars and had worked in a garage when I was in high school and junior college; so I was able to get the gas station on its feet easily enough. I'm also fairly handy with a hammer and nails and paint brushes and such and was able to do some remodeling, make the Welcome Inn less ramshackle, though rambling it would always be. At first I hired a woman away from a place in Lake Geneva to handle the hotel and restaurant, but she was a smart-ass, and eventually Linda took over.

Linda was no rocket scientist (I handled the books) but people liked her, staff and customers both, and she was damn near as good a cook as Wilma had been.

So my life had settled into something not unlike

normalcy. The vacation center we were a part of lent itself to water sports in the summer and skiing in the winter and there was plenty to do, including make a little dough at Wilma's Welcome Inn.

Both Linda and me got pudgy. Mine came from too much of her cooking, both at home and at the Welcome Inn, and from a general laziness—I ran the Inn like any good executive, delegating responsibility and filling my own life with relaxation. I listened to my stereo (Tony Bennett, Peggy Lee, Mel Torme) and read paperback westerns (they engaged my brain without taxing it) and watched old movies on TV (we had a satellite dish) and generally lived a life of leisure, acquiring the spare tire that went with it.

Linda's extra weight came from another source: my dick.

"You're pregnant?" I said.

"You sound...disappointed...or mad or something."

"Well, hell—how should I sound?"

We were discussing this at the A-frame, sitting out on the porch in deck chairs, looking out at a lake bathed in moonlight. Her eyes were a similar color—washed-out blue. I really liked the color of her eyes.

"You should sound happy," she said. Her eyes were tensing.

We hardly ever argued. In fact, I can't remember arguing with her. Sometimes I got mad at her when she was a little thick about some business aspect at the Inn, but when all was said and done, I cared more about her than any of that other shit, so I tended to cut her some slack. I mean, fuck, I didn't need the money. The Inn was just something to do.

"Happy isn't my style," I said.

"Sure it is," she said, and she got up and sat in my lap and smiled at me, dimples and all, though I could tell she was still sad.

"You want to break this damn chair?" I said.

She just smiled some more and hugged me around the neck and said, "I'm not that heavy yet. I'm only a month or so gone."

And she was a little thing, after all. I bet she didn't weigh a hundred pounds.

"I thought you were using something," I said.

"I was. I stopped."

"We should have talked about it."

"I thought you'd *want* a child with me. You said so once."

"I was drunk. And you know I don't drink, and when I do, I can't be held responsible."

"Well, you're responsible for this," she said, and patted her tummy, and her smile shifted to one side of her face, crinkling it.

Goddamnit, there's no way around it: I did love her, or as close to it as I'm capable.

I said, "If I was going to have a child, I'd want it with you."

"Well, I should hope to shout. I'm your wife, aren't I?"

"Only one I ever had," I said, which was a lie. I was

married one other time, but that was in another life, the life she didn't know about.

"We'll be a family," she said sweetly. "Won't that be wonderful?"

This girl thought life was a fucking Christmas card.

"Linda, I don't know about bringing anybody else into this goddamn place."

She looked confused. "What goddamn place?"

"This world. This planet. It's no prize."

"Our life isn't so bad, is it?"

"We have a great life."

"So, why not let a third person in on it? A person who's part of *us*, Jack..."

I shook my head. "You don't understand, kid. This is a very protected life we got going here. We're the couple in the plastic bubble—nothing touches us. But a kid—he's going to have to go out in that world and face all the bullshit."

"How do you know it's going to be a he? And what's wrong with going out in the world?"

"For one thing, it's crawling with people."

"I *like* people!"

"I don't. I'm not so sure pulling another passenger onto this sinking ship is such a hot idea. What's he got waiting for him? Or, her?"

She gave me a sideways look, trying to kid me out of it. "Don't be such a Gloomy Gus."

"Read the papers. They're full of famine and AIDS and nuclear bombs."

"Jack, you don't read the papers."

"Well, hell, I watch TV. And I've been out in that world, baby. It sucks."

"I don't know why you feel that way."

"Well I do."

"Why? Have you had it so bad?"

"Not lately."

She cocked her head, gave me a smirky, pixie look. "When did you *ever* have it bad?"

I tasted my tongue.

"I never mentioned it before..."

Her eyes narrowed. "What, Jack?"

"I...I saw some combat."

"Combat? Where?"

"Where do you think? In the war."

"What war?"

I sighed. "Vietnam, dear. A distant event in history that happened during your childhood. Let's just say...I'm not wild about bringing somebody into this life when Vietnams are still a part of it—and they are."

She looked very troubled. She was sweet but she wasn't deep. "I never heard you talk like this."

"Sure you have."

"Not so serious, at such length. I...always thought it was a joke, the things you say, the way you see things. You always made me laugh. It was just, you know...sick humor."

"Defense mechanism."

"What...what makes life worth living then?"

She was really getting upset; I decided to smile at her. Said, "Life's worth living as long as somebody like you's in it."

She beamed and hugged me.

I held her for a while. Listened to the crickets.

Then she drew away and said, "Jack, you don't really... you wouldn't have me get...rid of it, would you?"

Her lip was trembling and her china-blue eyes were wetter than the goddamn lake.

What else was there to say?

"Of course not," I said. "What do you think I am? A murderer?"

2

I was chopping wood, which was about as physical as my life got these days. The lake was placid and blue, surrounded by trees painted in golds and yellows and browns; the water reflected a soothing Indian summer sun. You could almost understand why somebody, long ago, chose to name the lake Paradise. There weren't even any mosquitoes this time of year.

I swung the axe in my two hands, building a rhythm, liking the pull on my muscles, enjoying the sweat I was working up, feeling alive. Wood chips flew and logs became firewood. When Linda got back from her yoga class at Twin Lakes, I'd prepare supper (still had a microwave) and the wine would be chilled and we'd sit before the fireplace and be "toasty warm" (as she put it) together. We would also undoubtedly have great sex, one of the major reasons I kept the ditsy little dish around.

Feeling winded but good, I sat out on the deck and unzipped my down jacket and relaxed with a cup of coffee. I was watching the lake when a cloud covered the sun and the gravel in my driveway stirred.

A chocolate BMW pulled abruptly up, making a little dust storm. I did not recognize the car—other than as the pointless and drab status symbol it was. I stood. My shoulders tensed and it had nothing to do with chopping wood.

From the edge of the deck I noticed two things: the driver of the car, a slightly heavyset man of about fifty in a London Fog raincoat; and the front license plate of the BMW, which was covered with mud. There hadn't been any rain in the Midwest for several weeks.

He saw me perched above him on the deck. My expression must have been hostile because he smiled tightly, defensively, and put both hands out, palms forward, in a stop motion.

"Just a few minutes of your time," he said, "that's all I ask."

He had a mellow, radio-announcer's voice and a conventionally handsome, well-lined face, a Marlboro man who rode a desk.

"Whatever you're selling, I'm not buying."

His smile twitched nervously. "I'm not a salesman, but I *am* here on business."

I motioned off toward the highway. "Talk to Charley up at the Inn. If he can't handle it, make an appointment to see me, there, later. I don't do business at home."

"This doesn't have anything to do with the restaurant business, Mr. Quarry."

I said nothing. A bird cawed across the lake. My sentiments exactly.

"I, uh, realize that isn't the name you're using around here…"

"Explain yourself."

The outstretched hands went palms up, supplicatingly. "Please. There's no reason to get your back up. There's no obligation…"

"You *sound* like a salesman."

"Your wife won't be home for another hour. I didn't want to bother you while she was here..."

Mention of Linda made me wince; this guy, whoever the fuck he was, knew entirely too much about me. He didn't know how close he was to spending eternity at the bottom of one of the area's scenic gravel pits.

"Come up here and have a seat," I said.

He smiled tightly again, nodded, and came around and up the stairs.

I sat in one of the lounge-style deck chairs, legs stretched out, and he took one of the director-style chairs and pulled it up near me. His salt-and-pepper hair was heavy on the salt and thinning a little, though some fancy styling minimized it; you could buy a week's groceries for what he spent on that haircut. He smelled of cologne—some expensive fragrance, strong enough to blot out that of the pines around us.

"May I smoke?" he asked.

"It's your lungs."

He lit up—something unfiltered from a flat silver case drawn out from under the London Fog; I had a glimpse of dark, vested, well-tailored suit with blue striped silk tie.

"I know this is an intrusion," he said, deferential as all hell, "but I think, when everything is said and done, you'll be pleased. This is the opportunity of a lifetime."

"Does this have anything to do with Amway?"

A short, harsh, nervous laugh preceded his response: "Hardly, Mr. Quarry. This is more on the order of... Publishers Clearing House." The constant if slight smile turned wry, smug. "Mr. Quarry, I'm in a position to make you a very wealthy man."

"Drop the name, all right? I haven't used that in almost ten years."

He made a small open-hand gesture. "A man known as the Broker gave it to you, a long time ago."

"That's right." I looked at him, locked his eyes. They were gray, like his cigarette smoke. "What else do you know about me?"

His smile faded, and he shrugged facially. "I know that you were a hero. That you served your country honorably and well."

"Yeah, right. Is there more?"

"I known that you were married once before. You returned from a tour of duty in Vietnam to discover your wife had been untrue."

"Untrue? I found her in bed sitting on a guy's dick."

"You killed him."

I shrugged. "Not on the spot. I came back the next day, after I cooled off, and he was under his sporty little car, making some minor repairs. I made one, too."

"You kicked the jack out."

I shrugged again. "He called me a 'bunghole.' What would you do?"

"You were arrested."

"But not tried, except in the papers."

"The unwritten law."

"There are two times society puts up with murder."

"War is one," he said, nodding.

"Finding somebody fucking your wife is the other."

He gestured with cigarette in hand. "Nonetheless, you were looked down upon in certain quarters."

"I had trouble finding work. I was a Vietnam vet, remember? We were all assumed to be unreliable dope addicts. And I was a 'disturbed Viet vet' before it was fashionable. Before it was a cliche even."

I killed a guy, after all. Nobody minded the numerous yellow people I killed for no good reason. The one white asshole I killed for a good reason got people bent out of shape.

"Shortly after that," he said, carefully, quietly, the gray eyes studying me but pretending not to, through a haze of cigarette smoke, "you met the Broker."

"Did I?"

"I don't know the circumstances, but you began taking contracts. Working as part of a team."

Did I mention I had brought the axe up on the porch with me? Well, I had. It was leaned up against the front of the house, near the door. Not far away at all.

"Are you sure," I said, with a gentle smile, "that you want to keep this line of conversation going?"

"I just want you to know that I'm familiar with your background."

"Why?"

"Because I have a contract for you."

"I'm not in that line of work anymore."

"Mr. Quarry, you are an assassin. It's not something you can leave behind."

I nodded. "Well, I'm willing to kill again, under certain circumstances."

"Such as?"

"Assholes coming around fucking in my life."

He smiled again, another tight nervous twitch, and he said, "I'm not here to make trouble in your life. I'm here to improve your life."

"Say it. Whatever it is you've got to say, say it."

"Mr. Quarry, this isn't something one can…"

"Say it. I sat through 'This Is Your Life' patiently enough, but now the show's over. Cut to the commercial."

He cleared his throat, as if about to make a speech. Maybe he was. "You are said to have been the best at what you do. But you dropped out."

"I dropped out. My partner bought it, the Broker bought it, and I dropped out. Say what you came to say."

He let the cigarette fall to the deck and ground it out with his heel.

Then he said: "One million dollars."

There's only one thing you can say when somebody says that, and I said it: "What?"

"One million dollars," he repeated.

"In regard to what?" I asked, dumbfounded and a little annoyed.

"One contract."

"A million-dollar contract."

He nodded, his smile confident now, not nervous at all. "One hundred thousand down. In cash. Unmarked twenties. It can be delivered to you in twenty-four hours."

"I'm...retired."

"I noticed you hesitate before saying so."

"Anybody would hesitate, offered a million bucks."

"You could go anywhere in the world. You and your wife. Nothing could touch you."

"Don't mention my wife again."

"No offense meant."

"Don't mention her. Don't speak of her. Or I'll cut your fucking heart out."

He swallowed and nodded. He'd noticed the axe.

"I just wanted to emphasize what a rosy future you could paint for yourself with that kind of money."

"I don't believe in the future, and I don't give a fuck about the past. And my present is rosy as fucking hell. So why don't you just go away."

"Mr. Quarry, it's a million dollars."

"I know it is. But...I'm retired. What do I need with it?"

"One job. One simple job."

"I doubt it would be simple."

"You'd be surprised."

I stood. I walked to the edge of the deck and looked out at the lake. The sun was still under a cloud and a light breeze was blowing in. The water looked gray. I was going to have a son, or a daughter, before long. With my past, maybe it would be a good thing to get out of this country. With a million bucks you could live like a king in Mexico or South America. Maybe on a beach, the ocean your front yard. A protected life. A safe life for me and mine. In a year, I would be forty years old.

I turned and looked at him. "What's the contract?"

"Have you heard of Preston Freed?"

"I've heard the name...he's some sort of right-wing loon, isn't he?"

His face cracked with the first of his many smiles to reveal teeth; too white and too perfect to be real.

He rose and walked over to me. "That's exactly what he is," he said, folding his arms, seeming at ease with me for the first time. I'd have to do something about that. "He is the founder and leader of the Democratic Action party."

I made a sound in my throat that wasn't quite a laugh. "Just another one of these homegrown would-be Hitlers."

He shook his head no. "He's not a Nazi. His politics are a grab-bag mixture of extreme right and extreme left, but he's relatively young and genuinely charismatic, a Kennedy of the lunatic fringe if you will...and he's gathering real momentum for his movement. Do you follow the political scene in the papers?"

"I catch it on TV. But, look..."

He raised a hand in a gentle stop motion. "Freed has several key issues that have rallied conservatives around him—he's strongly anti-abortion and pro-school prayer, for instance. That's all some people need to hear."

"I suppose, but..."

"You don't have to know much about politics to understand that the coming presidential election will be a volatile one. We have a once popular, now somewhat tarnished president ending his two terms in office. Supposedly a conservative, this man has raised the national debt to a record high."

"Politics don't interest me."

"Even so, we are coming into a fascinating election year. The two parties—depending upon whom they choose as their standard bearers of course—should be in for a real battle. Think of it: the highest office in the land up for grabs…we could have a true conservative in the White House, or our most liberal president in years…"

"What does this have to do with anything? If this contract is political, you can really forget it."

His gray eyes pleaded with me, his brow knitting a goddamn sock. "Mr. Quarry, Preston Freed is a presidential 'spoiler' in the truest sense. The way his movement, his 'party,' is gathering steam, he will throw the entire election off kilter."

"Yeah, I suppose. I don't know much about it, and I don't want to, either."

"At this point, it is hard to say whether the Democrats or the Republicans would suffer the most, but…"

"I think you should leave. This is a civics lesson that I just don't want to hear."

"I represent a certain group of private citizens, responsible, powerful, patriotic citizens, who want Preston Freed stopped. Who want the natural order of our political system restored, and this madman—this potential American Hitler, as you aptly described him—destroyed like the rabid animal he is."

"That's very colorful, but I don't do politicals. I don't do *any* contracts anymore, as I tried to make clear…and I shouldn't have let you get into this at all."

"Mr. Quarry…"

"I don't do windows, and I don't do politicals."

"Why not?"

"You can offer me two million and I'd turn you down."

He was astounded; shaking his head. "Why, do you think it would be difficult to get near the candidate? True, Freed is somewhat reclusive, but with the first primary in January, there'll be plenty of opportunities, starting with a major press conference next month, which…"

"Stop. It's not hard to kill a politician. It's the easiest thing there is. You got a public figure, an egomaniac who thinks he's immortal, going out kissing babies and shaking hands and it's the easiest hit in the world."

"Then what is your objection?"

"I wouldn't live to spend the money."

"Are you implying that…"

"That you would have me killed? Why, I don't know what got into me. You and your concerned patriotic citizens wouldn't *think* of being party to murder, now would you?"

"Mr. Quarry, we are men of honor."

"Sure. I'd be an instant loose end, pal. You don't get away with shooting presidents or even would-be presidents. Oh, the guys who hire you can get away with it. In fact they always do. That's 'cause the poor bastard who squeezed the trigger is either dead or locked in a cell and written off as a madman."

"I assure you..."

"I'm retired. I don't want to get back in the business, not even once, not even for your big bucks. This is a real good place to call a halt to this conversation...I still don't know your name, and that's how I like it."

"You won't reconsider?"

"No. And I don't want to see you again. You know far too much about me. I ought to kill you on general principles."

He sucked breath in, hard; till now, talk of death had seemed abstract to him, I'm sure. "But...but you won't."

"Not unless I see you again."

He nodded, sighed, extended his hand for me to shake. I ignored it.

Withdrawing the hand, he smiled gently and said, "No hard feelings, Mr. Quarry. It's too bad. I think you'd have been the right man for the job."

I didn't say anything.

His smile disappeared and, shortly, so did he, in a cloud of gravel dust; the BMW's back license plate was covered with mud as well.

I went inside and started a fire.

I sat before the glow of it, by the metal conical fireplace in one corner of the A-frame's living room, and waited for Linda, wondering if I should've killed the son of a bitch.

Quarry's Story Continues
In Thrilling New Novels

QUARRY'S EX

by **MAX ALLAN COLLINS**

HOMICIDE BEGINS AT HOME

Every hitman finds his way into the job a different way. For Quarry, it began the day he returned stateside from Nam to find his young wife cheating. He'd killed plenty overseas, so killing her lover was no big deal. And when he was recruited to use his skills as a contract killer, that transition was easy, too. He survived in this jungle as he had in that other one—by expecting trouble.

What he didn't expect was ever running into *her* again…

PRAISE FOR MAX ALLAN COLLINS

"Crime fiction aficionados are in for a treat… a neo-pulp noir classic."
— Chicago Tribune

"Collins never misses a beat…All the stand-up pleasures of dime-store pulp with a beguiling level of complexity."
— Booklist

"Max Allan Collins [is] like no other writer."
— Andrew Vachss

Available now from your favorite bookseller.
For more information, visit
www.HardCaseCrime.com

Quarry's Story Continues
In Thrilling New Novels

QUARRY'S CHOICE

by MAX ALLAN COLLINS

QUARRY TAKES ON THE DIXIE MAFIA

Quarry is a pro in the murder business. When the man he works for becomes a target himself, Quarry is sent South to remove a traitor in the ranks. But in this wide-open city—with sin everywhere, and betrayal around every corner—Quarry must make the most dangerous choice of his deadly career: *who to kill?*

PRAISE FOR MAX ALLAN COLLINS

"Collins breaks out a really good one, knocking over the hard-boiled competition (Parker and Leonard for sure, maybe even Puzo) with a one-two punch: a feisty storyline told bittersweet and wry...the book is unputdownable. Never done better."
— Kirkus Reviews

"An exceptional storyteller."
— San Diego Union Tribune

"Rippling with brutal violence and surprising sexuality...I savored every turn."
— Bookgasm

Available now from your favorite bookseller.
For more information, visit
www.HardCaseCrime.com

Quarry's Story Continues
In Thrilling New Novels

THE WRONG QUARRY

by **MAX ALLAN COLLINS**

A HIT–AND A MISS...

Quarry doesn't kill just anybody these days. He restricts himself to targeting other hitmen, availing his marked-for-death clients of two services: eliminating the killers sent after them, and finding out who hired them...and then removing that problem as well.

So far he's rid the world of nobody who would be missed. But this time he finds himself zeroing in on the grieving family of a missing cheerleader. Does the hitman's hitman have the wrong quarry in his sights?

PRAISE FOR MAX ALLAN COLLINS

"A suspenseful, wild night's ride [from] one of the finest writers of crime fiction that the U.S. has produced."
— Book Reporter

"A sharply focused action story that keeps the reader guessing till the slam-bang ending. A consummate thriller from one of the new masters of the genre."
— Atlanta Journal Constitution

Available now from your favorite bookseller.
For more information, visit
www.HardCaseCrime.com